Drive Me Crazy

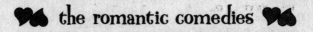
the romantic comedies

Drive Me Crazy

ERIN DOWNING

Simon Pulse

New York London Toronto Sydney

This book is a work of fiction. Any references to historical events, real people, or real locales are used fictitiously. Other names, characters, places, and incidents are the product of the author's imagination, and any resemblance to actual events or locales or persons, living or dead, is entirely coincidental.

SIMON PULSE
An imprint of Simon & Schuster Children's Publishing Division
1230 Avenue of the Americas, New York, NY 10020
Copyright © 2009 by Erin Soderberg Downing
All rights reserved, including the right of reproduction in whole or in part in any form.
SIMON PULSE and colophon are registered trademarks of Simon & Schuster, Inc.
Designed by Ann Zeak
The text of this book was set in Garamond 3.
Manufactured in the United States of America
First Simon Pulse paperback edition June 2009
10 9 8 7 6 5 4 3 2 1
Library of Congress Control Number 2008050195
ISBN: 978-1-4169-7484-0

For Henry and Ruby.
May you always be surrounded
by love, laughter, and tasty treats.

Acknowledgments

This book wouldn't exist without my sparkly new editor, Anica, who has marvelous suggestions and anecdotes that make writing much more fun.

And, as always, thanks to Greg—who gives me very clever plot ideas, and who washes the dishes while I write.

Prologue

Love, Wisconsin

The first kiss tasted like toasted marshmallows, the sweet and sticky flavor of a summer bonfire. His mouth was soft and warm from days spent outside in the sun at the lake. As they kissed, his hand traced a line up her spine, twisting her insides into spirals. She melted into him and thought about their summer together, weeks of flirting and teasing that had finally progressed to a real kiss on their last night together.

He pulled back and looked at her, his piercing green eyes cutting through the dark night. A smile tugged at the corners of his mouth. It was the same look he'd given her all summer—but this time it was different, because now she knew where things stood. They had kissed. There was a new kind of bond between them, the kind of connection she'd seen played out in movies and the "Your Stories" section of her favorite magazine. She sighed, as she knew she should, and he leaned in for another taste. When he pulled away, she felt her lips hang on, sticky with marshmallow.

But in one tiny second the moment of bliss turned to a scene of horror. His hands gripped her arms and his eyes snapped open. His look was no longer teasing; it was terrified. "Kate, my lip is stuck in your retainer."

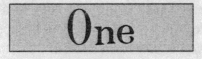

One

New Jersey

Gasp! Kate Rogers's mouth snapped closed and her eyes popped open, suddenly awake. A tiny trail of drool had begun to escape from her mouth, and she swept the back of her hand across her chin to dry it.

It was the last day of school, so study hall was essentially empty. The few people who had bothered to show up for last period were stealthily sending text messages or paging through magazines while Mrs. Coyle pretended not to notice. Kate was there only because she'd feel guilty if she skipped . . . even on the last day of school, when she had nothing to study.

Kate glanced around the room to try to figure out who'd seen her napping. As usual Curtis Chin was watching her from his table across the room. Curtis was a very nonthreatening type of creepy. Kate shot him a look, and he eagerly waved at her. Kate was glad Curtis was graduating. She had lucked into study hall with him every semester since ninth grade, and his apparent attraction to her hadn't faded.

Curtis's crush wasn't flattering, since he also harbored an unrequited crush on Kate's best friend Alexis Goldstein, and had gone so far as to send snail mail *letters* with his drawings of fairies and dragons to her other best friend, Sierra West. Sierra had graciously thanked Curtis for his kindness and artistry, and had gently explained that he wasn't her type; Alexis had just growled at him to "get lost, freak."

A quick peek at her watch told Kate there were only six minutes left in her junior year of high school. She pulled a magazine out of her bag and flipped through it absent-mindedly, thinking about the dream she'd just had. The marshmallow kiss, the feeling of Lucas's hand tracing its way up her spine, the look in his eyes.

This wasn't the first time Kate had fallen asleep in study hall, and it definitely wasn't the first time she'd had that dream. The scene was always the same, an exact replaying of the moment she and Lucas had shared at the end of last summer. In real life, the kiss had been perfect, but the ending was a different version of awful each time she relived the moment in her dreams. Once, Lucas had pulled away in a dream because Kate's dad had been standing next to them singing "Itsy Bitsy Spider." Another dream had ended with Alexis and Sierra both watching their kiss from a judging table, holding up scorecards. (She'd gotten a 4.4 out of 10.)

This time she wasn't sure what the deal was. . . . Kate hadn't worn a retainer during the day since eighth grade. (She still wore it while she slept, which is something only Alexis and Sierra knew about.) She imagined these freak-out dream endings were just her nerves acting up, wondering what would happen between her and Lucas this summer. They had ended things with such a magical moment at the end of last summer, and had been exchanging flirtatious e-mails and IMs all year. She couldn't wait to see him in person in less than a week!

The bell rang, signaling an end to study

hall, eleventh grade, and Kate's years with Curtis Chin. Kate smiled thinly at Curtis as she passed him on her way out the door, then breathed a sigh of relief that he was out of her life for good.

Now that the school year was through, she was just days away from reigniting the fire that had started to simmer last summer. As they had every year for the past ten years, Kate and her family and friends would be spending the next month and a half at the Cattail Cottages Resort in Love, Wisconsin (pronounced Loave, Wis-*can*-sin, which amused Kate tremendously). This year Kate would finally live out her dream of spending the summer kissing and whispering under the big pine tree, and she couldn't wait.

Kate grabbed her bag out of her locker and slammed the empty metal cavern shut with a hollow thwack. She had left only a small piece of notepaper tucked into the far back corner, with a tiny "hello, you, from kate" scribbled on it. Kate did this every year—a message-in-a-bottle-style greeting to whoever moved into her locker the following fall.

Kate was a true romantic, and liked to think that the future inhabitant of her locker would find her note and track her down, and he would end up being the love of her life. This romantic scenario hadn't yet played out (in fact, this past year Curtis Chin had moved into Kate's old locker, and the secret note had only fueled the fire of his crush), but she left a little greeting again this year anyway, just in case.

Someday her prince would come.

"Kat!" Alexis hugged her from behind and pushed her toward the front doors. "We're seniors, Kat! Yaaaaaaah!" Alexis pumped her fist in the air, her long almost-black hair swinging out behind her.

Alexis had called Kate "Kat" since fourth grade, after Kate had hastily climbed up—and even more quickly gotten stuck in—a tree, and the fire department had had to come and help her down with their big ladder. Just as the nickname had started to fade, in the middle of fifth grade Kate had scratched Justin Thornton when he'd called Sierra "chubster" on the playground. Justin had sported a cat-scratch-like mark for about a week, and Kate's nickname had stuck with Alexis ever since.

"Woo-hoo!" Kate cried, hopping off the last two steps toward the front lawn of campus. She and Alexis skipped outside with the rest of the student body, everyone celebrating their summer freedom. It was a muggy New Jersey spring afternoon, and people had rolled up their jeans and sleeves to enjoy the sunshine.

Kate and Alexis sprawled out on the school's lawn to wait for Sierra, who was probably bidding each and every teacher a personal farewell. Sierra did those sorts of things, which is certainly why she was so successful at everything she did. Sierra had just won student council president for the upcoming school year, and she was pretty obviously going to get valedictorian next year as well. She'd been given the honorary faculty prize in this year's awards assembly, earning her a thousand-dollar college scholarship, compliments of the local business association.

In spite of her good-girl seemingly perfect exterior, Alexis and Kate loved her anyway. They knew the real Sierra, and she was a lot more fun and interesting than her campaign posters would suggest. "Hey, bitches." Sierra had slid up behind her two friends on the lawn and whispered this in their ears. Ms. Mohan passed them at that moment and flashed a wave of hello. "Have a fantastic summer, Ms. Mohan!" Sierra said as she waved, dripping candy sweetness from her sugary smile. Then she turned to her friends and said, "Let's get this party started!"

Kate grinned. "Eighteen hours until the girls' road trip hits I-80!" she announced, pulling Sierra's slides off her slender feet for her. Then she unsnapped her bag and pulled a list out of the interior pocket. "I think we're just about ready. Are our road trip tunes set?" she asked.

"Check," Alexis declared, tapping her iPod inside the back pocket of her jeans. "My road trip playlist is so hard core that you will puke before we get through every song. And I'm making us listen to it until we hit Ohio, just for fun."

"Snacks?" Kate asked. Her stomach rumbled at the thought.

"Swedish Fish and Diet Cherry Coke!" Sierra clapped. Sierra was a total snack fiend, which you would never guess from her looks. Her "chubster" nickname was long forgotten. . . . She was now as long and willowy as a professional ballet dancer. Her dark skin glowed from within, as though she only ate spinach salad and water. Kate, on the other hand, was average height, "curvy" (Kate called herself "stocky," which was far from the truth), and subject to skin disturbances every time she approached a french fry or processed sugar.

Kate studied her road trip prep list, growing more excited. For the first time ever, this summer the girls' parents were letting them drive themselves to Love, and they had been planning their road trip for weeks. "And I have the entertainment covered," she concluded. "Quizzes from the last six months of four different magazines, maps, travel and accommodation guides—"

"Ooh," Alexis cut in sarcastically. "Fun!"

"Bite me," Kate cheerfully shot back, then continued. "—And a detailed map of every possible amusement park along the way, including one that has one of those freaky fortune-telling machines."

Sierra waved at a few girls from her AP history class, then turned back to Kate and Alexis. "I am so excited about this trip, y'all." Sierra had lived in Birmingham, Alabama, until third grade, and tiny little bits of the South still popped up in her vocabulary every now and again.

"Me too," Kate agreed. "My two best friends, the open road, a cute boy waiting for me at the end . . ." Not to mention that the road trip across country with her two best friends meant that she didn't have to sit in the back row of her parents' minivan with her little sister for the almost twenty-four-hour drive to the lake house. And Lucas's warm, tan, scrumptious body was the pot of gold at the end of the road! "I had my dream in study hall again," she said, lying back on the grass and looking up at the big oak tree hanging over them. "This time Lucas's lip got caught in my retainer." She cringed at the thought of Lucas's perfectly smooth, scrumptious lip tangled in her mouth gear. Eek.

"By the time you finally get some, you're going to be so freaked out that you won't remember how to kiss," Alexis said, and rolled her eyes. "You'll see him in a week, Kate. We have almost a week of girl time ahead of us—please tell me that the whole trip won't be consumed with romantic speculation about your upcoming summer o' love."

Kate smiled at her. "In fact," she said smugly, "I had planned to talk about Lucas every single moment of each of those days, if you don't mind."

Alexis hopped up onto her knees and leaned over Kate, her scrawny 104-pound frame silhouetted by the sun above her. "I do mind. I think we're all pretty clear about exactly what happened last summer—your 'magical' kiss"—Alexis wiggled her fingers in the air—"and it's obvious exactly what needs to happen this summer. I have made it clear that you just need to jump him when we get to the lake, and everyone will live happily ever after."

"Okay, okay," Sierra cut in. "Alexis, you must be patient. Kate is preparing for her romantic rendezvous with her summer crush, and it's our job to be supportive and talk her through it." She smiled at Kate. "We know Kate wants the big moment to be perfect, and I'm willing to help with that. On the other hand . . ." She furrowed her eyebrows. "The Lucas talk better stop by the time we get to Pennsylvania, or there will be no Swedish Fish for you. Enough is enough!"

Kate frowned at both of them. But in all fairness she knew she'd been yammering on and on about Lucas for almost eleven months. She was ready to get some action, and wanted to stop talking about it just as much as her friends wanted her to. But Kate also wanted to make sure that everything was perfectly planned out, so her reunion with her hot soon-to-be-boyfriend would be as magical as their farewell night together the previous summer.

Lucas and Kate had been building a serious flirtation for almost three years—ever since Lucas's family had started renting a summer cabin at Cattail Cottages—so their first kiss had been a major milestone. Their online flirtations all year suggested he was as ready as she was to take things to the next level as soon as they were together again. Lucas and his family were flying in his dad's private plane from Winnipeg, Canada, in two days, and were scheduled to be in Love a few days before Kate, Alexis, and Sierra rolled in. Just enough time for him to build up the appropriate level of longing for the moment Kate would arrive.

"I don't know how you've waited a full year to get some," Alexis declared, settling into a cross-legged position on the grass. "I'm dying, and I saw Kevin when he was home for spring break." She blew her long bangs away from her eyes. "I don't think our one-day stop is going to be enough time to catch up, if you know what I mean." She giggled mischievously.

Sierra looked at Kate, her eyebrows raised dramatically. Kate laughed, then said, "We get it, Lex." One of the benefits of the girls driving separately from their parents was that they could stop to visit Alexis's boyfriend, Kevin, at the University of Michigan en route. He had just finished his first year of college and was planning to stay in Ann Arbor for a summer internship. Alexis had decided to surprise him with a quick visit.

"I packed my boob shirt," Alexis announced proudly, just as Mr. Prince, their English teacher, walked past. He covered his ears and cringed. "Sorry, Mr. Prince. Have a good summer!"

"Nice, Alexis," Kate chided. She abruptly changed the subject away from Kevin. Sierra and Kate thought Alexis's boyfriend was a creep. Sierra could hold her tongue, but Kate preferred to avoid the subject since she rarely had anything nice to say and often blurted out something she would later regret. "Sierra, is your mom staying the whole month?"

The Rogers, West, and Goldstein families spent the summer together at Cattail Cottages Resort. Greg Rogers, Cynthia West, and Sara Goldstein worked as professors together at the university in their town, and for the past eleven years each had taken at least a month off after classes ended to relax and read academic papers by the lakeshore in Wisconsin.

Alexis's family had found the resort—she and her cousin Adam's family had started going there together when they were babies—and had convinced the West and Rogers families to join them one summer when there was availability in the neighboring cabins. It had become a tradition, and now every year the whole crew caravanned from New Jersey to Wisconsin as soon as school let out.

This summer the university had finished finals a week earlier than the high school, so the Rogers and West families had decided to leave for the lake a little early, after agreeing that the girls could drive out on their own. Alexis's parents weren't leaving until next week . . . most likely so someone's parents were still around to keep an eye on things until the girls' road trip motored off to the west.

"My mom is playing it by ear," Sierra responded quietly. "She's not sure how long she's staying. I think she has a lot going on in the lab this summer, but I'm sure she's a little freaked about committing to a whole month with my dad."

"Are they still in the test phase?" Kate asked. Sierra's parents had been separated off and on for the past year, and had only just recently returned to "half-on."

"Yes," Sierra muttered. "Their new therapist is big on 'demonstrating your feelings,' which means they're constantly kissing and hugging and rubbing each other's hands. It's completely disgusting, and Sasha and I are both concerned that a summer cooped up with them in a tiny little cabin in the middle of nowhere could be brutal."

Alexis chuckled. "Perhaps they'll consider your feelings before demonstrating theirs when it's just the four of you in two small rooms."

Suddenly a soccer ball landed in the middle of the three girls, leaving a muddy print on Kate's road trip prep list. "Yo, pass that back!" A guy with dark, shaggy hair snapped his fingers. All three girls just looked at him. "Hello? Toss me my ball."

"Adam, you kicked it at us. Walk over here and get it yourself." Kate lay on her back in the grass, idly watching the clouds. Adam was Alexis's cousin, and Kate had known him for years. Not only were Adam and his two brothers over at Alexis's house most weekends, but Adam's family also rented one of the cottages at Cattail Resort every summer.

When they were younger, Kate and Adam had actually sort of been friends—especially during their time at the lake. Their idea of fun almost always overlapped, and he used to be downright hilarious. But as the years had passed, his humor had turned to arrogance, and what used to be fun just came across as rude and inappropriate the older they got.

The end of Kate's patience came in sixth grade, when Adam spread a rumor around their new middle school about Alexis sleeping with a whole collection of Barbie dolls every night. (Which was only a little bit true. . . . It was just Malibu Barbie and a Ken doll, but the specifics were irrelevant.) Alexis was tortured for the first three weeks of school, and most people called her Baby G for the rest of the school year. She hadn't been able to shake the nickname until she'd started dating—and kissing—Kyle Stevenson, the captain of the football team, and he'd forced people to shut up already.

Kate hated Adam for ruining her friend's reputation (if only temporarily), but also because Adam was a prick with a serious sense of self-righteousness, and a bossy, argumentative streak that bothered her immensely.

Out of the corner of her eye Kate watched Adam lift his eyebrows and move toward them to get his ball. "Okay, Kate, if you want to be a bitch about it, that's the way we can play it." When Adam reached the edge of their circle, he didn't stop moving. He stepped on Kate's stomach and walked over her. He grabbed his ball, turned, and lifted his foot to step on her again.

Kate sat up, grateful for her Abs of Steel workout video, and nimbly grabbed Adam's ball out of his hands. Ignoring the muddiness, she shoved the ball inside her shirt and declared, "*This* is the way we can play it, Adam." She held her arms across her stomach and shoved her bag into her lap to hide the ball. She knew she was being childish, but her adrenaline had kicked into high gear. She *hated* Adam and was sick of the way he always did whatever he wanted to. "Now, run back to your friends and find a new game. We're through with you here."

Alexis and Sierra exchanged a look. They knew Kate was stubborn, but they both knew Adam was just as much so. This war could go on for hours. With a tiny little smirk Alexis leaned back to watch the drama unfold. Sierra looked mildly uncomfortable but was clearly enjoying the scene.

"I see," Adam said, crossing his arms over his chest. "So you're telling me that you like my ball inside your shirt? You'd like to keep it there?"

"All I said," Kate spat back at him, ignoring his totally lame attempt at sexual humor, "is that you can run along now." She held her hand up like a stop sign and yawned. "You're boring me." Kate was mortified at the way she was acting. She sounded like a third grader . . . or like Adam. He totally brought out the worst in her.

"Well, this should make things a little more interesting for you," Adam said. He grinned, bent down, and pulled Kate's bag out of her lap. In the single moment it took for this to happen, Kate lost her concentration. So when Adam's hand reached up her shirt and pulled the ball out, she just sat there staring. "I hope that was fun for you," Adam said. "Since *that* was one sexy move, and probably the only action you'll get this summer." With a wink and a snap of his fingers he trotted off to rejoin his buddies, leaving Kate, Alexis, and Sierra staring after him.

Kate felt her skin burn where he had touched her. Her heart was racing, and the anger bubbled up inside. Had it been anyone other than Adam, she would have been blushing. Because as far as Kate was concerned, there was nothing sexier than a good, well-fought fight.

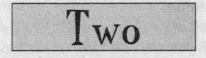

Two

On the Road to Pennsylvania

The next morning Kate stood outside her house with her duffel bag by her side. She'd been packed for weeks and couldn't stand the wait for even one more moment. Alexis had planned to pick Sierra up at her house. Then they would head to Kate's before motoring off to the west in Alexis's little green Ford.

Kate stood in her driveway, growing agitated for no reason at all. She had come outside more than ten minutes before her friends were supposed to get there, and couldn't blame them for the fact that she was still waiting. She reached into her bag to grab her cell phone to check the time, and realized it wasn't there.

Crap. She'd left it plugged in over-night, and had forgotten to grab it from the kitchen counter before she'd locked up. She pulled out her keys and let herself back in. The phone was right where she'd left it the night before.

She had six new text messages and a voice mail. Before she could look at her messages, she heard Alexis's horn sigh in her driveway. The horn sounded like a dying cow suck-ing its last breath, and Kate chuckled as she slipped her phone into her pocket and hur-ried out the door.

Sierra waved to her from the front seat, and Alexis leaned her head out the open driver's side window. "I'm driving first shift so I can control the tunes, yo."

"You can drive every shift, babe. I will man the navigation." Kate swung her bag into the trunk and moved around to the back door. She stopped short when she real-ized the backseat wasn't empty. "What are you doing here?"

Sprawled across the backseat, one foot lounging into Kate's space, was Adam. He was drinking a bottled Frappuccino, and a little bit spilled as he shifted to make room for her next to him. Kate leaned into the window to glare at Alexis. "What is he doing here?" The panic was evident in her voice.

"Dude, why didn't you call me back?" Alexis swiveled in her seat. "I called you last night, and texted you, like, eight million times."

"I didn't get the messages." Kate was staring at Adam suspiciously. His precious soccer ball sat in his lap, taunting her. Her skin crawled at the memory of what had happened the previous afternoon. "Does anyone want to tell me what's going on?"

Adam put on a fake smile and—in a ridiculous Valley girl accent—said, "Like, I'm coming with you!" He clapped. "Road trip with the girls!" His face turned expressionless. "Yes, that's right, Kate. You and I will enjoy the magic of each other's company for the next"—he looked at the clock on the dash of the car—"one hundred twenty-six and a half hours in this car—approximately."

Kate shot a desperate look at Alexis, who glanced in the rearview mirror, and then said, "Adam has a scholarship interview at the University of Michigan. He has to be there on Monday afternoon, and Aunt Michelle can't leave Jersey until Sunday. My parents knew we were planning to stop to see Kevin in Ann Arbor anyway, so they made me bring him with us. They insisted he didn't need to take the skanky bus when we were going to the exact same place."

Sierra leaned her head out the window. "Come on, Kate, just get in." Kate scowled at her before reluctantly sliding into the open spot next to Adam.

"I may have come across as genuine a few moments ago, when I jumped for joy about this road trip." Adam adjusted his position so he was taking up as much of the backseat as was humanly possible. "But let me tell you that I'm looking forward to crashing your road trip just slightly less than you ladies are looking forward to having me here. But fate aligned and brought us all together, so I think we should make the most of it."

Alexis rolled her eyes and signaled to turn onto the interstate. They were on their way. All four of them. As Kate turned to look out the back window to watch their hometown shrink into the distance, Adam said, "So, who wants to play truth or dare?"

When they stopped at a gas station in the middle of Pennsylvania for toilets and treats four hours later, Kate was convinced that she had died and gone to hell. Absolutely everything she had envisioned for their girls' road trip had soured into a giant disappointment.

Alexis was snippy (she refused to wear her glasses, and straining to see highway signs had given her a headache); Sierra was distant and quiet (Kate knew her parents' split was bugging her, but Kate couldn't talk to her about it with Adam lurking around); and Adam was rude, sarcastic, and condescending (translation: asshole). As far as Kate was concerned, the start of their highly anticipated road trip had been four of the worst hours of her life. She'd spent most of them folded into her corner of the car, trying to put as much distance as possible between her body and Adam's.

"Only one toilet works, so we'll have to flip to see who gets to test the waters." Adam was swinging a giant rubber fish with a key attached to it. He had been sent inside the gas station to find out where the loo was located. "I, personally, am relieved that I stand to pee."

"I'll go first." Kate rolled her eyes at Adam and grabbed the limp fish from his hand. "I brought seat covers."

"Of course you did." Sierra laughed. "I'm coming with you."

"Me too." Alexis grabbed Kate's hand. "See ya, Adam. Girls pee with partners."

When they were safely out of earshot, Alexis blurted out, "What's with you, Kat?"

"What do you mean?" Kate pulled out a tissue to open the door to the bathroom. The knob was grimy, and pieces of the tissue stuck to the metal when she twisted her hand away.

"I mean, why are you being so abrasive to Adam? What's your deal with him?" Alexis held the door open, and Sierra and Kate followed her into the restroom. The smell of cigarettes and sanitizer was overpowering. The size of the room made the disgusting toilet cowering in one corner look miniature. There was a machine on the wall dispensing Purple Passion condoms, and next to that was a wooden sign that said: WOMEN ARE LIKE FISH: THE BIGGER, THE BETTER.

"My deal is he bugs me. He's rude, arrogant, and is ruining our road trip."

Sierra held her hand out for a seat protector, which Kate proudly pulled from her bag. "Ladies, turn away. I'll go first." Sierra laid the thin piece of paper over the toilet seat and groaned when it soaked up little wet puddles that had been camouflaged on the black seat. "This is disgusting—I'm squatting."

Alexis and Kate turned to face the condom machine to give Sierra some privacy. Alexis nudged Kate's foot with her own. "So you're saying that you are already convinced you're going to have a crap time on this trip, just because Adam is here?"

"Do you feel like things are off to a great start?"

"No, but I think that's because—" Alexis cut off as Sierra flushed the toilet with her foot.

Sierra piped up from behind them. "Because you're being a brat, Kate. Do you need to be so argumentative? I mean, he asked if anyone was hungry this morning, and you told him you'd rather starve than share his bag of pretzels. That's just sort of mean. I know he's not your favorite person, but maybe you could give him a chance, and see if things could be a little more . . ."

"Fun for everyone?" Alexis finished.

"So now it's my fault that our *girls'* road trip is ruined?" Kate couldn't decide if she wanted to scream or cry. How could her friends not see her side? "You're saying that since I think Adam is annoying, I'm the one ruining the trip?"

Alexis moved toward the toilet for her turn. "God, this is gross. No, Kat, that's not what we're saying. I guess I'm just wondering why he bothers you so much. You're not usually like this, and he's not *that* unbearable."

"You know I've hated him since middle school. And now he's always just such a prick that I can't really get past it. Lex, I can see why you deal with him—he's family. But, Sierra, doesn't he get under your skin?"

"Come on, Kate." Sierra washed her hands in the filthy sink, lifting her long, slender leg up to turn the faucet off with her flip-flop when she'd finished. "You know I don't let him bother me. He actually sort of cracks me up, if you want to know the truth."

"Dude, how did you do that?" Alexis was referring to Sierra's leg-faucet trick. "Kat, maybe you're just being a little bit dramatic? I've forgiven Adam for the Barbie doll rumor. . . . You should too."

"I'll do my best to be civil," Kate said as she moved to take her turn at the toilet.

"But I can't promise anything. I don't like when people mess with my friends, which he did, and you guys are just going to have to deal with that. I'll try to get over it, but unless he starts to act less like the asshole that I'm certain he is, then this car ride will be a little hostile."

"Kat: the defender of my reputation!" Alexis laughed, turning a quarter into the Purple Passion machine. "How effective can a twenty-five-cent condom be? This place freaks me out." She pulled the lavender package out of the dispenser and set it on top of the machine. "Free protected sex, courtesy of Alexis Goldstein. Some creep will find this later and it will make his day."

"So generous, Lex. I'm glad you're looking out for the people of Wherever-we-are, Pennsylvania," Kate said, and then giggled as she washed her hands. When she'd finished, she gestured to Sierra to bring her leg over to turn off the faucet with her foot again. Sierra happily obliged. Then the three girls hustled out of the bathroom to give Adam his turn.

When he emerged from the bathroom thirty seconds later, Adam was waving something in his hand as he strolled back to the car.

"Check it out!" he called, grinning widely. "Purple Passion!"

Kate, Alexis, and Sierra looked at one another and all burst out laughing. For the first time all day Kate felt like there could still be hope for their road trip after all.

Late that afternoon, somewhere on the other side of Pennsylvania, the girls decided it was time to call it a day. The sun would be going down soon, and they had passed a sign that said there was a campground a few exits up the highway. They had a tent, and were excited to use it. Most of the motels they'd passed that they were able to afford were far creepier than a tent, anyway, and camping was much more fun.

Adam had volunteered for a shift as navigator and was holding the atlas upside down—just to be funny—and calling out random directions every time they passed an exit. Kate was driving, and found Adam's map humor to be about as amusing as Mr. Tannen's famously painful history class. But Sierra's constant giggling was egging him on, and Alexis periodically chimed in by loudly reading the billboards they passed. Kate felt like the only outsider, which made

Adam seem even more annoying.

"Seriously, Adam, can you please just pay attention and figure out where we're going?" Kate slammed her hand on the steering wheel, startling Alexis out of her zoned-out state in the backseat.

Adam laughed. "Geez, Kate, chill. Take the next exit, and then trust me. . . . I'll get us there."

"I'm sure," Kate grumbled, then stuffed a handful of Swedish Fish into her mouth to keep from saying what she wanted to say.

Adam leaned across the front seat and studied the dashboard. "Hey, daredevil, you're really risking it driving fifty-five in a sixty."

"Adam . . . ," Alexis warned sleepily from the backseat. Things hadn't gotten a lot friendlier between Adam and Kate over the course of the day, and Alexis and Sierra had started to mediate. Adam had started to push Kate's buttons just for the fun of it. He seemed to get a thrill from pissing her off.

Adam grinned. "This exit, please."

Kate signaled to exit, and followed Adam's direction to take a left off the exit ramp. They drove for nearly ten minutes down a narrow, empty road in silence. The only sound was a periodic shuffling of paper when Adam adjusted the map. "How much farther?" Kate asked eventually. "I'm starting to get a little freaked out. This sort of feels like the setup for a horror movie."

"I think the map might be outdated," Adam responded. "We should have been there by now."

"Give me the map," Kate demanded. She slammed her foot on the brake and pulled to the side of the road. She glanced at the atlas and said, "We should have gone right off the exit ramp. We're going in the wrong direction." She shoved the map at Adam, put the car back into gear, and pulled a U-turn.

Ten minutes later they pulled into the campground, which was less than a mile off the interstate the *other* way. As they drove through the park searching for a spot to call home for the night, neither Kate nor Adam said a word.

Three

Pennsylvania

"Since you can't find your way around a map, I'm quite certain you'll struggle to figure out how to put a tent together," Kate said, and then smirked.

Alone with Adam, Kate was free to vent all of her frustrations toward him without her friends getting uncomfortable. Sierra and Alexis had set off in search of dinner food, and had left Kate and Adam to set up the tent. Kate wanted to do it herself, but Adam had insisted he needed to stay to help. As if.

"Well, now," Adam muttered under his breath, but loud enough for Kate to hear. "Those are fighting words."

Kate fixed him with an evil look and muttered right back, "What did you expect, loving glances and doting compliments?"

"Hey," Adam shot back, "you don't need to be snobby about it. We're going to be together twenty-four-seven for the next few days, so maybe you could try to be just the tiniest bit civil, instead of an evil bitch from hell?"

"That doesn't even deserve a response," Kate retorted. "Are you going to help me put this tent together, or would you just like to sit on that log over there and enjoy a cool soda while I show you how to be useful?"

"You are feisty, aren't you?" The look on Adam's face suggested he was sort of enjoying their banter. "So you're saying you need a gentleman's help?"

"That would be great," Kate stated calmly. "I'd love to have a gentleman's help. Unfortunately, I have to use you instead. Can you please contribute for approximately thirty seconds?"

"Yeah," Adam said, surrendering. "Of course I'll help. It would have been easier if you'd asked nicely. Possibly a 'pretty please'?"

Kate wanted to scream. Adam clearly thrived on pissing her off. Opting to ignore him, she pulled the pieces of the tent out of their nylon bag and started laying them on the ground in straight, orderly piles. Long stakes, short stakes, sections of tent fabric. Once everything was out of the bag, Kate stepped back to survey the project. Three neat stacks of tent parts, all straight and organized.

Adam was watching her with an amused smile. "All set?"

"Yes, thank you." She looked at him suspiciously. "Why are you looking at me like that?"

"Would it bother you if I, say, did this?" Adam reached his leg out and pushed one of the tent stakes with the toe of his shoe. The stake was now lying at a ninety degree angle to the other stakes and looked completely out of order.

Kate reached her shoe out and pushed it back into place, neatly next to the others.

"It does bother you, doesn't it?" Adam chuckled.

"No," Kate insisted. She didn't want to let Adam know that disorder bothered her immensely. "You bother me."

Adam started laughing harder now. "That's becoming clear."

Kate pulled the tent's assembly instructions out of the bag and squatted down to start to put the pieces of the tent together. "Step one . . . ," she muttered, grabbing a couple of pieces off the ground.

"Why are you doing it like that?" Adam asked, squatting down next to her. "These pieces go here." He pushed two long poles together. "See? Like that."

"You're supposed to put this part together first." Kate pulled the pole apart and adjusted it slightly. The way Adam had put them together would maybe have worked, but it wasn't the way it was supposed to be done. *She* had the instruction booklet . . . not him. "*Then* you can push these two poles together."

"Oh, I see." Adam nodded. "So even though the end result is exactly the same, the way you've done it is right, because you're incredibly bossy and stubborn and want to be difficult?"

"Or maybe it's because I have the instruction booklet and don't want you to assemble a tent that's going to fall apart on us during the night? Fine, I'll just let you put all of these poles together. Let me know when they're done. Don't screw it up."

Kate stormed off and grabbed their tarp out of the trunk. She laid it down on a flat part of the campsite that looked like a good place to set up the tent. It was right next to the campfire pit, which seemed like it would help keep the tent nice and toasty if the air cooled off overnight. She could feel Adam watching her as he put the pieces of tubing together. "Do you have something else to say?"

He held his hands up in front of him defensively. "Nope. By all means, keep doing what you're doing."

"What's wrong with the way I'm doing it?"

Adam surveyed the tarp and glanced around the rest of the campsite. "I guess I was just thinking we could put the tent up back there," he said, and gestured to a tall stand of pine trees that had a gorgeous, soft-looking grassy space in the center. "But if you want to sleep right next to the fire and hope the wind doesn't blow the fire onto the tent and burn us all up in the night, by all means . . ."

Huffily, Kate grabbed the tarp and pulled it across the campsite to the stand of pine trees. Adam had made his point, and she decided it was easier not to argue with him. Maybe if she ignored him, he'd just go away.

After a few glorious minutes of silence while they each worked independently, Adam had all of the tent poles assembled and Kate had the tarp laid out. She had put rocks on each corner of the tarp to keep it in place. Adam brought the long poles over, and Kate dragged the pieces of tent fabric.

"So next," Kate said, pulling the instruction booklet out of her pocket, "we put these little stakes into the ground to hold the corners of the tent in place."

Adam paused, then said simply, "Okay."

"Do you have a different idea?" Kate could tell he was questioning her logic. It was the way he'd said "okay" with a totally non-okay tone.

"I think we need to put the long poles through the channels before we secure the corners—that way we know how big the tent will actually be."

Kate was boiling with frustration. Adam was *so* bossy and couldn't stop acting like a tent know-it-all. In truth she had never actually *been* in a tent before, but there was no way she was going to admit that. Instead she said simply, "I have the instruction booklet, Adam. So let's do it the way it's supposed to be done." She hated the way he brought out this side of her. She knew she was being completely confrontational and argumentative, but the way he criticized her every move was infuriating.

After a few false starts the center of the tent eventually lifted into the air. It wobbled slightly in the evening breeze, but stayed upright. "That looks about right," Kate declared, stepping back to admire her work.

"Nicely done," Adam complimented. She realized he was being genuine, and swelled with pride. "Let's get our gear inside," Adam instructed. "It's getting dark, and we should get things ready before Lex and Sierra get back with dinner."

"Don't we need to finish securing the tent first?" she asked, studying the instruction manual.

Adam shook his head. "No, we can do that afterward. As long as it's up, we're fine pulling our gear inside." Kate shrugged and tossed the instruction manual outside the door of the tent. She'd let Adam have his way this time, since things seemed to be going okay. *No thanks to him.*

They walked together back to the car. Kate popped open the trunk and pulled her big duffel bag out. "Do you want me to get that for you?" Adam offered.

"I can handle it," Kate snapped back. *Now he's trying to be helpful?* she mused. When they got back to the tent, Kate climbed in with her bag and Alexis's sleeping bag. Once she'd finished arranging Alexis's spot in the center of the tent—next to Adam, who was on the far wall—she unzipped her big bag and started to pull out her pillow.

She had just lifted her pillow to fluff it when suddenly the center of the tent made a snapping sound and the whole thing came billowing down around them. "Ayeeee!" Kate shrieked, buried in the mounds of tent fabric.

"You okay?" Adam cried from somewhere nearby, under the fallen fabric.

"I'm buried alive!" Kate declared, then burst out laughing. Adam cracked up too, and they both started flailing around in the tent trying to find an escape route.

"Stay still and I'll try to get it back up again. There's no sense in both of us risking our lives to dig out of here," Adam joked. A few moments later he was standing in the center of the tent fabric with the posts back in place. Kate applauded from her seat on the ground. Adam shrugged. "I guess you were right. . . . We should have secured it a little better before we started to get our stuff inside."

Thank you, Kate mused silently. *Ha, ha! I was right!* Out loud she said, "No biggie. If you hold it up for a sec, I'll get the final stakes in place and we should be back in business." She went outside the tent and quickly read through the rest of the instructions. After she placed the stakes, she was confident that everything was in order. She ducked back inside the tent and started to get her bedding out.

"Did you bring a *duvet*?" Adam was rolling his thin sleeping bag out on the floor on the other side of the tent, but had stopped to watch what Kate was doing. "Please tell me that's a duvet."

"It is. Why is that funny?" *Here we go again*. Kate had started to consider that maybe Adam wasn't as intolerable as she had thought, but now she suspected things were about to sour again.

"Princess, we're in a tent. You don't bring a duvet to go camping." Adam was cracking himself up. "Did you bring your hair dryer and tanning oils as well? Do you need me to pick up your mattress from the front desk? Shall we call for room service?" Adam held his hand up to his ear like a phone and spoke in a fussy accent. "Yes, yes, I'll take the lemon verbena hand massage and a salmon salad, thank you."

Kate narrowed her eyes at him but kept her mouth shut. It wasn't worth engaging with him further. Once she had her sleeping space in order, she turned to Adam and blurted out, "Can you get out of here? I need to change into my pajamas."

"Are you going to bed? What about dinner?"

"I'm not hungry."

"Don't you need to brush your teeth or anything?"

"Is that any of your business?" Kate wanted him to scram. She just wanted to change and go through her nighttime routine in silence and privacy. She hadn't even thought about how they would get ready for bed and change and all the other things you just *do* in front of your girlfriends but that seem especially private and embarrassing when there's a guy nearby. She noticed that her retainer case had fallen out of her pajama pants pocket, and she quickly shoved it deep inside her pillowcase away from Adam's prying eyes.

"Brushing your teeth is not my business," Adam responded, just sitting there, completely disrespectful of her wish that he leave her alone. "But it will be my business when you're breathing dragon breath all over the car tomorrow."

"Ugh, you're such a pig!" Kate cried out.

Adam grinned, the way he always did when Kate started getting loud and angry. "Sorry."

"If you're really sorry, you'll get the hell out of this tent immediately. I just want to go to sleep, and I want to do that without you staring at me like some sort of creep. Tell Lex and Sierra good night. I'm sure I'll be up first in the morning, so I can drive first shift."

Kate zipped the tent shut after Adam crawled out, closing the door on her terrible day. It couldn't be over soon enough.

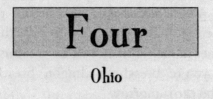

Four

Ohio

—

By noon the next day everyone was in a foul mood and ready to stop for lunch. They'd been driving since before eight that morning, and they were all tired and at one another's throats.

Alexis and Sierra had apparently gotten lost on their way to find a grocery store the night before, and hadn't gotten back to the campground until almost eleven. Adam had sat up waiting for them next to a crackling fire—Kate had been able to hear his banjo strumming quietly as she'd tried to fall asleep. As annoying as Adam was, he had a beautiful voice, and his singing had helped her drift off into slumber. Of course, the thought of seeing Lucas in a few days had kept her tossing and turning. Her imagination was running wild and kept her up far longer than she would have liked.

"Lucas texted me this morning and said we should go to this huge amusement park that's about thirty miles off the next exit, if anyone's up for it," Kate offered hopefully. They were a full day and a half into their trip, and so far, they weren't having a lot of fun. A roller coaster could put a smile on anyone's face, she figured.

"Well." Adam slapped his knee. "If *Lucas* suggests we all go there, then by all means we should!"

"What does that mean?" Kate whipped around from her front seat to glare at Adam in the back. Adam and Lucas knew each other from summers at the lake, but they'd never really been friends. Lucas hung out with his brothers and a couple other guys whose families owned cabins near the Cattail Cottages Resort. Adam had always been buddy-buddy with the guys who worked at the resort during the summer. Totally different crowds.

"I think an amusement park sounds fun," Sierra cut in.

Alexis nodded her agreement. "Let's do it.

We're ahead of schedule, anyway, so we have some time to kill. Adam's interview isn't until tomorrow afternoon, and we're only a few hours' drive away from Ann Arbor."

"But Kevin awaits you in Michigan, Alexis. Don't you want to keep on truckin'?" Adam pulled a twine of licorice from the bag that was resting between Kate and Sierra. "Thanks."

"Kevin is at some sort of orientation training session thing this weekend. He's not getting back until late tonight, and I want to make sure he's there. So no rush. Tomorrow's good." Something in her voice sounded strained, and Kate made a mental note to ask her what was going on later. Later, when they could get rid of Adam.

Half an hour and no further conversation later, they pulled into the amusement park parking lot. "Fifteen dollars for parking?" Kate exclaimed. "That's insane." She was tight on cash for the road trip, and couldn't stomach spending that much to park. They still had to pay the entrance fee!

"I can cover it," Alexis said quickly, and Kate knew it wasn't worth further discussion. Alexis was in a different financial position from Kate, and it was stupid to pretend otherwise. Kate didn't have a lot of money to spare, unlike Alexis, whose family seemed to be made of money. Alexis got to pick a car for her sixteenth birthday; Kate got dinner out at the steak and sushi place near her house.

The difference in financial status sometimes caused tension in their friendship, but usually Alexis was pretty good about not treating Kate like a charity case. Kate was pretty frugal all year long, since she gave up the chance to get a summer job in order to spend every June and July at the lake. During the school year they usually just hung out at someone's house, and it helped avoid uncomfortable money situations.

As Sierra eased Alexis's car through the line toward the parking lot booth, Adam announced, out of the blue, "I just realized I forgot a shirt for my interview. Why don't I just drop you off here, and I'll hit that mall we passed a few miles up the road. Pick you up in a few hours?"

Kate couldn't hide her enthusiasm at the idea of getting a few hours alone with her girlfriends. "Sounds great." *Dumbass*, she thought. *What kind of loser forgets his shirt for such an important interview?*

"You're going to the mall instead of a roller coaster?" Alexis chided. "Pick us up by that big elephant over there, okay?" She pointed to a giant green elephant near the entrance to the park. "Say, four o'clock?"

"Right." Adam saluted at Alexis. The girls hopped out of the car, and Adam jumped into the driver's seat. He did a quick U-turn and sped off, as though he couldn't get out of there fast enough.

"He seems to be having a lovely time on our road trip," Sierra joked as Adam drove off.

"Hmm," Alexis mused. "Maybe not so much. But *we* didn't invite him to ride across the country with us, so I'm not too worried about it." She pulled several twenty-dollar bills out of her wallet and hastily paid the entrance fee for all three of them. "My treat. . . . Please accept this as my apology for us getting stuck with my cousin on our road trip."

Kate smiled appreciatively. *Count on Alexis to find a way to pay without making me feel like a total mooch.* "Thanks. You don't have to do that, though."

"It's the least I can do. But he's not all bad, is he?" Alexis looked at her friends hopefully, clearly feeling guilty about their trip going awry.

Sierra replied, "Not at all. Adam cracks me up."

At exactly the same time Kate declared, "Ugh. He's so annoying!"

Alexis laughed. "Two very different opinions."

"I'm sorry," Kate said, and she meant it. She didn't mean to complain about Adam, but he was just so obnoxious and rude. She continued, "He wasn't even willing to read the instruction booklet about how to put the tent together last night, so it collapsed on top of us. And he totally mocked my duvet, which was just childish. It's not *that* funny that I brought a duvet, is it? Just because he has a ratty old sleeping bag, somehow he's, like, Captain Camping, granted full liberty to criticize the way I packed for a road trip or something?" Kate stopped for a breath, and both of her friends cracked up laughing.

"Why is that funny?" Kate asked, starting to laugh herself. "Okay, so he irritates the hell out of me. I guess you get it? Plus, what an idiot. . . . Who forgets to pack their shirt for a scholarship interview? It's the whole point of him being here."

"He's afraid of heights," Alexis said, shrugging. "I think he used the shirt as a less-embarrassing excuse to avoid the roller coasters."

Sierra laughed. "He couldn't get out of here fast enough. I was wondering what was going on. Aww . . . It's Adam's sweet, vulnerable side. Poor guy."

Just then Kate's phone beeped, signaling a new text message. From Lucas.

"Ooh!" Alexis declared. "Is that from Prince Charming, who will greet you at the end of the road with a big fat smoochy kiss?" She grabbed Kate's phone and flipped it open, reading the message aloud: "'Just got to Love. How long till you get here? It's not as fun without you.' Aww! He's so sweet." She rolled her eyes and tossed the phone back to Kate, who reread the message and melted a little.

"Okay. Now I want to skip the rest of the road trip and just get there already," Kate confessed.

"Hey, now!" Sierra scolded. "Y'all need to remember that this summer is just as much about the road to Love as it is about Love itself. This is *our* adventure."

Alexis lifted her eyebrows. "With all

that Love in there, you sound like Kate, Sierra."

"What's wrong with being a romantic?" Kate protested.

"All right, all right," Sierra mediated, as she often did when both Kate and Alexis started to show their stubborn streaks. "Do you guys want to get a picture?" They were just inside the entrance to the park, and people were stopping in little groups to have their pictures taken as a souvenir of their trip to the amusement park.

"Oh, yeah!" Alexis grabbed both of her friends around their waists and grinned at the greasy guy behind the camera. The photographer complimented Alexis on her smile, which cracked them all up. Kate looked at Sierra, and they both stuck their tongues out at the same time.

The photographer checked his work and gave them a thumbs-up. "Perfect!" he cried, then kissed his fingertips at them.

"Icky," Sierra observed quietly. They made their way over to the printing station, where all the recent pictures were displayed on a big screen. Their picture wasn't posted yet, so they scanned the other pictures that had been taken. There was a funny shot of a bunch of white-haired old ladies, all making faces at the camera. One of the ladies was doubled-up with laughter because another was tickling her side as the photographer captured the shot. "That's priceless," Sierra declared, pointing at the photo.

"Of course, I peed my pants a little when she tickled me," said a voice behind them. One of the old ladies from the picture was standing behind Sierra. She chuckled, then pointed at the picture screen. "Now, that's a cute one. You girls look like you're having fun."

The picture of Alexis, Sierra, and Kate had just been posted on the screen. Sierra and Kate were grinning at each other with their tongues out, but their bodies were only half in the picture. Apparently, the photographer had been a little too excited about Alexis's smile. It was a great shot nonetheless. "Yeah," Kate agreed. "We *are* having fun."

"Good," the lady responded, then rubbed Kate's shoulder. "Girlfriends are the spice of life. Even when they torture your weak bladder." She chuckled, then sashayed off with the picture of her and her friends, waving the photo in the air for them all to see.

Kate watched as the group of old ladies giggled about the picture and teased one another about the way they looked. As she stared at them walking off into the amusement park, having a great time, Alexis dangled a photo key chain in front of her face. "I bought one!" she announced. "We'll share it."

An hour later they had gone on the big roller coaster three times. Every time they got in line, they found themselves behind the same group of old ladies. They'd discovered the women were on a bus tour around the Midwest. There were forty of them in total, and they were louder than a high school volleyball team on their way to an away game. Kate, Alexis, and Sierra could hardly talk while they waited in line, since the tour bus gang was so chatty.

Kate felt the buzz of a text message in her pocket during their third ride on the roller coaster. After they piled out, she pulled her phone out and checked it. Lucas again.

"What did he say?" Sierra prodded.

"He just said he's getting ready for the barbecue, and wishes we were there tonight." Kate blushed, thrilled that Lucas seemed to be on exactly the same wavelength that she was on about their summer together. She was glad she had the road trip to hang out with Alexis and Sierra, since she was getting the impression that Lucas wanted her all to himself when she got there.

Alexis rolled her eyes, prompting Kate to ask, "What's your deal, Lex?"

"You're so delusional about your so-called relationship with Lucas."

"What is that supposed to mean?"

"It means, you're bound to be disappointed." Alexis said this harshly, clearly intending to hurt Kate's feelings. "I wish you would just live in the present and not fantasize about some perfect relationship with a fantasy guy you barely even hooked up with a year ago."

"Lex," Sierra warned, "don't bring your own relationship issues into Kate's romance."

Alexis narrowed her eyes at her friends. Then tears sprung to her eyes, and she quickly turned away from them. Kate reached out to grab her arm, and Alexis pulled away. "What's going on?" Kate asked gently. "Lex, are you okay?"

"I'm just being stupid," Alexis grumbled bitterly. "Let's get cotton candy, okay?"

Sierra laughed. "Air-spun sugar is not going to distract us. We *need* to know what's eating you."

"Fine," Alexis relented. "But I still want cotton candy."

Kate bought a bag of blue, purple, and pink cotton candy, and they all settled on a bench overlooking the water ride. It was oppressively hot, and the periodic splash of the water at the bottom of the track was refreshing.

Alexis dipped her hand into the bag of sugar and said, "I guess I'm just angry at Kevin for not coming home at all this summer. I'm at the lake for the first part of summer anyway, but then I'm stuck in Jersey without a boyfriend the entire month of August. I feel like he should want to be with me, but he's doing this whole internship thing instead." Alexis paused to let a piece of cotton candy melt on her tongue. She rolled her tank top up at the bottom, exposing her flat stomach to get some sun. "I know it sounds selfish, and I guess I should have known this was coming, but I'm not sure I'm ready to deal with whatever it is we have to deal with now that he's all into his college life and I'm, well, not."

"Lex, that's not selfish," Kate said seriously. "It's fine to want to see your boyfriend. You're soul mates, right? So it's important to spend time together."

Alexis laughed loudly. "Soul mates? I don't know about that. It's more like we hook up and have a good time."

"Come on," Kate insisted. "There has to be more to it than that. You're in a *relationship*. If he's not giving you the attention and respect you deserve, you need to find someone who will. You owe it to yourself." Kate knew Kevin would never treat Alexis the way a boyfriend should. He was a jerk with his own agenda, and she wished Alexis could see that. But she also wanted to be supportive of Alexis's choices.

Sierra had been sitting quietly, biting off bits of blue cotton candy. Finally she broke in, "You two have to realize that you're looking for totally different things with relationships." She let the sugar melt on her tongue, then continued. "Kate, you're looking for storybook romance and a guy who treats you like the leading lady in a romance movie. Lex, you're looking for, um . . ."

"Are you trying to politely say that Kate is a hopeless romantic and I'm just hopeless?" Alexis offered this suggestion jokingly, but Sierra clearly felt bad.

"No! I'm just saying that Kate's fantasy of what it is to be a girlfriend is very different from your reality."

Alexis shrugged. "Yeah, I guess. And you know what? If things don't work out with Kevin, I'll find another guy. I always do." Then she smiled brightly, prompting Kate and Sierra to both crack up laughing. "Now, who's up for another ride?"

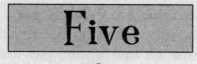

Five

Ohio

The interstate stretched out in front of them, semis whizzing by with a loud *fwump* every few minutes. Kate had taken over in the driver's seat when Adam had picked them up at the amusement park, and Adam had insisted that he should sit in the navigation seat to prove that he wasn't an idiot with the map. Kate had relented, but only after both Alexis and Sierra had begged to take the backseat so they could nap.

Now her best friends were soundly asleep, awash in slanted early-evening sunlight, and Kate was stuck with only Adam to keep her company. In an unfortunate case of bad luck, the AC in Alexis's car had decided to take a siesta of its own shortly after they'd left the amusement park, so all the windows in the car were down. The temperature had crept up to near ninety, so they were all sweating and miserable. But at least the open windows provided enough noise that she and Adam didn't really need to have a conversation. They sort of had to yell over the noise of the wind and the highway to hear each other.

Adam was playing basketball with a tiny suction cup net and foam ball he had bought at the mall that afternoon. He had the net affixed to the dashboard, and was throwing the ball from a semi-reclined position in the front passenger seat. He was about 0 and 60, since the wind whooshing through the car was blowing most of his shots off track. Kate was mildly amused, watching him struggle to land a single shot. But Adam didn't seem fazed by his lack of skills. . . . He just kept trying, clearly enjoying the little game he'd devised for himself.

Finally his shot went straight into the net, and Adam lifted his arms into the air. "That was hot. Snap!"

"Snap?" Kate mocked loudly. A truck

whizzed by, its giant tires roaring next to their window. "Seriously? Snap."

"What?" Adam asked, leaning toward Kate so she could hear him. "I can't say 'snap'?"

"You can. If you want to sound like a freak."

"Why is 'snap' freaky?"

"It's not. It's just out of place on you." Kate thought for a second. "It's a little like you saying something's hot, unless it's a direct comment about a girl. And since you just called *yourself* hot, I guess you're oh-and-two in the normal department."

"Hold on," Adam said, and fiddled with the glove compartment, opening and closing the latch, making his net flip up and down. "You think I'm abnormal?"

Kate shrugged. She could see Alexis stir in the backseat, but she stayed asleep. "I think you're sort of a jerk, but I guess that's still considered normal, right?"

"Oh, that's nice," Adam replied. "So I'm a jerk, and you're a real delight? A lovely girl with absolutely no inner bitch, right?"

"Did I say that?" Adam was totally right, and she was willing to admit it. "I have plenty of inner bitch. And you're adept at bringing her out to play."

"Well, aren't I a lucky guy?" Adam said sarcastically. "A special part of you is reserved just for me? That's awfully romantic."

Kate looked over at him, disgusted. "I'm not trying to be romantic, so if you're getting romance vibes from me, your intuition is in serious need of repair."

Adam flopped back in his seat, grinning. "Aren't you glad I'm on this road trip?"

"No."

"Admit it," Adam encouraged. "I amuse you."

"Um, no."

"Then I'll keep trying," Adam said seriously. "It might take time, but I'll crack through." Kate ignored him. It was easy to do.

They sat without talking. Adam studied the road atlas while Kate memorized highway signs advertising IHOP and gas stations. "I'm dying," Kate declared suddenly. The sun had gone down, but still there was no relief from the heat. Kate's hair was in two braids going down either side of her neck, and little beads of sweat were traveling down her exposed skin. "No AC is torture."

"Take this exit," Adam announced, grinning mischievously. Kate looked at him quizzically. "Just take it. There's a pretty big town near this exit. Let's go swimming."

"Where?"

"We need to find a country club," Adam answered. "They have the best pools."

"How are we going to get into a country club? They're members only."

Adam grinned mischievously. "You're so focused on the rules all the time, Kate. You're missing out on all the fun in life. We'll figure out a way in."

"Where are we?" Sierra mumbled sleepily from the backseat about twenty minutes later. "How long did I sleep?"

They had just pulled into the parking lot at a super-ritzy country club that Adam had located on Alexis's iPhone. He'd stolen it out of her purse while she slept, Googled "country clubs" in the area they were driving through, and successfully navigated to a wealthy-looking town about fifteen miles off the interstate. Kate couldn't deny the fact that she was impressed.

"Oy," Alexis groaned crabbily. "I'm hot."

"Kate and I have masterminded a very

clever plan to remedy that," Adam bragged. "Who wants to go swimming?"

"Nuh-uh," Alexis said, and shook her head. "These roadside motel pools are nast. I wouldn't put my foot in, even if I already had a toe fungus."

Adam tsk-tsked at her. "You are such a snob, Lex. What would you say if I told you we were going swimming at a country club?"

"And how are you going to swing that?"

"Like this." Adam hopped out of the car and walked toward the gate that led into the club. It was just after nine, and the sign said the country club had closed at eight. They all followed Adam as he moved alongside the fence that divided the interior of the club from the parking lot, and down into a little marshy area that took them back out along the main road.

Silently they walked along the road for about a hundred yards. There were no cars, and it was getting dark, so Kate started getting freaked out. They could go missing, and no one would even know where to find them. "I don't think this is a great idea," Kate said finally. "You don't even know where you're going, Adam."

In response Adam just held a finger to his lips and cut back in from the road, leading them through a thick patch of trees. The branches and pine needles bit into Kate's arms, and just when she thought she could go no farther, the trees opened up onto a grassy golf course. Off to their left they could see the big clubhouse, its exterior lamps lighting up the night sky. They walked up the fairway together.

"If I were a betting guy, I'd put money on the pool being in there," Adam said as they got close to the clubhouse. He was pointing to a rectangular area that was closed in with wide-plank wooden fencing. The top of a lifeguard chair was poking up over the top of one section of the fence.

Kate pulled her flip-flops off her feet and carried them as they walked toward the pool. Her feet were sore from their day at the amusement park, and the cool grass felt amazing. Her whole body was sticky and hot, and she was momentarily tempted to lie on the grass to cool off.

As they approached the pool, Kate's hopes fell. She could see no obvious way to get inside the fence. Alexis slid down on the grass to rest while Adam scoped out the perimeter. Sierra and Kate both watched nervously for any signs of authority. Neither of them was particularly good at breaking the rules, and—to Kate at least—all of this felt a little risky.

"The gate is locked," Adam declared.

Kate stared at him, dumbfounded. "Did you think it would be open?" she asked. "That was your plan?" She was no expert at sneaking in, but even she could have told him the gate would be locked.

"*No*, that wasn't my *plan*. But I figured it couldn't hurt to check." He fixed Kate with a frustrated look, then his face broke into a goofy grin.

Why does he stare at me like that? Kate wondered. *It's like he's trying to annoy me and knows his stupid grinning makes me want to slap him.* But the way Adam made Kate's blood boil was invigorating, and she had to admit that she sort of enjoyed sparring with him.

There was a golf cart parked next to the fence. Adam climbed onto the hood. He lifted one leg up onto the roof of the cart and hoisted his other up onto the top of the fence. He dangled there for a minute, then flipped his other foot effortlessly over the edge and lowered himself down so only his fingers were in view over the top of the fence.

Kate, Sierra, and Alexis watched from the ground, listening for a deadly thud on the other side. Adam's whoop of success told them he had landed in one piece. Finally Sierra vocalized the thing they were all thinking: "How are *we* supposed to get over?"

"Sierra, you could make it . . . but there's no way I'm tall enough," said Alexis.

"Quit your nay-saying, Cousin," Adam said, as his head poked over the top of the fence. "We're all going swimming." He lifted a lifeguard's rescue ladder over his head and twisted it in midair to lower it down on their side of the fence. "Thanks be to lifeguards. Who wants to go first?"

Kate bravely stepped forward to the ladder. Her foot touched the bottom rung, and she got a shiver of excitement. She'd never really broken the rules before, and she was in the process of breaking and entering. She realized it was the most harmless kind of trespassing, but still . . . they could get caught!

Another foot, then another, and suddenly she was at the top. Adam was smiling at her, and when he grabbed her arm, she felt incredibly safe. He held her hand to help her over the top of the fence, then guided her hips as she settled her feet onto the ladder he was standing upon on the other side of the fence.

Kate tensed up. There was something in his touch that was so reckless, yet so gentle, that she shivered in the hot night. It was a momentary thing, but Kate was shaken by it nonetheless. Adam usually made her boil with frustration, but this time the feeling was different. When she hopped off the last rung of the ladder on the pool deck, Adam lifted his hand to give her five.

"Nice effort, princess! Good to see you're able to have a little fun, even though we don't have an instruction manual." Then he winked, and climbed back up the ladder to help Sierra over.

Kate instantly hated him again. She couldn't believe she'd started to warm up to him just because he'd helped her over a freakin' fence! As though he was some sort of Prince Charming, coming to rescue her. *Whatever.* They didn't need him to have fun, and they didn't need his help to break into the pool. They could totally have done this without him. *Just because he wrapped his hands around my hips, I don't need to be all charmed by him*, Kate reminded herself.

"I'm so glad Adam is here," Sierra said breathlessly when she stepped off the ladder. "This is exciting!"

Kate pretended she hadn't heard her, because she didn't want to acknowledge that Sierra was right. They would, of course, have been having fun, but they probably wouldn't have been sneaking into a country club pool to cool off. Adam did bring a level of excitement to their trip that she wasn't sure they would have achieved without him.

Kate surveyed the pool area. There were two separate swimming spots: one that was shallow for little kids to wade in, and another that was deep and dark and refreshing-looking. There were padded lounge chairs all around the edge of the pool, and little cabanas in each of the corners. A concession stand stood next to the entrance gate and was stocked with sodas (behind locked refrigerator doors) and boxes of candy bars.

As soon as Alexis had been safely shepherded down the lifeguard's ladder, Adam grabbed the ladder he had propped on the exterior of the fence and secured it back on its stand alongside the interior wall. No one would ever know it had been moved. Then he plunged, fully clothed, into the deepest part of the big pool. He pulled off his wet shirt and whipped it onto the pool deck, narrowly missing Kate. She, Alexis, and Sierra sat together on the edge of the pool, dangling their feet in the water.

"Ohhhh." Alexis sighed. "This feels amazing. I'm going in." Then, with her tiny little shorts and T-shirt still on, she lowered herself down into the pool and dog-paddled around before finally submerging to swim the rest of the width of the pool underwater.

Sierra was next. She pulled her skirt off (it was from Anthropologie, and probably wouldn't have fared well in chlorine) and wore just the bike shorts she had on underneath and her tank top. She eased herself into the water and dipped under.

"You're all alone out there," Adam said to Kate, paddling over to her on the edge of the pool. "After all the hard work of busting in, don't you want to swim?" She did, but she didn't have bike shorts on like Sierra, and she wasn't wearing short shorts like Alexis. Ridiculously, she was wearing jeans—which helped explain why she had been so hot all day. If it had been just her girlfriends, she'd have happily gone in the water in just her skivvies, but with him there—not so much.

"I do, but . . ." Kate didn't really want to tell Adam why she hadn't yet joined them in the pool. He'd already made fun of her for being such a priss, and she didn't really feel like ruining the evening by fighting with him again. But if he started teasing her, she knew she'd be pissed, and that would be the end of the fight-free period.

"But what? You don't want to come in naked, eh?" Adam was smirking again, which started Kate's blood boiling. "Oh, don't get feisty. I'm just teasing you. I bet you look great naked."

Before Kate could get mad, Adam splashed her, which cooled her off tremendously. Then he grabbed his wet T-shirt off the pool deck and set it next to her on the edge of the pool. "Wear this," he suggested. "It will be like a dress on you. Then you can come in and play with the rest of us."

"Okay," Kate agreed. She slipped inside one of the cabanas and pulled her hot jeans and tank top off. Adam's shirt was soaked and chilly, but it felt great against her toasty skin. The T-shirt hung down to Kate's midthigh—perfect. She ran out of the cabana and jumped straight into the pool. "Ayeee!" The water was colder than she'd thought it would be, and it felt amazing.

They bobbed around in the pool for a long time. Kate and Sierra easily beat Alexis and Adam at a game of chicken, knocking Alexis off Adam's shoulders in about five seconds flat. Alexis and Sierra settled into padded lounge chairs on the side of the pool, watching Adam and Kate do flips into the water. Kate had mastered the art of flips during their summers at the lake. Her little sister had taught Kate all her figure skating jumps and spins. Kate couldn't stay upright on skates to save her life, but she could execute all the moves perfectly when she did them off the dock.

Just as Adam hit the water with a loud thwack—his triple spin had gone awry and had turned into a basic cannonball—Sierra's cell phone rang. Sierra shushed them all and flipped her phone open to answer it.

"Hey, Mom," she said innocently. "Yeah, we're having a great time. We just got to our hotel for the night. . . . No, it's pretty nice. It has a pool." She smiled at the others, holding her finger to her lips while her mom talked on the other end of the phone. "No, Mom, don't do that. . . . It will get easier. . . . Please. I'll be there in a few days." She paused again, and they all sat silently, listening to Sierra's end of the conversation. "Can you just try? For Sasha. . . . Okay, I'll see you in a couple days. . . . I love you, too. Say hi to Daddy."

She closed the phone, and exhaled a huge sigh. "Everything okay?" Kate asked.

"Yeah," Sierra mumbled. "My mom is threatening to go back to Jersey."

"Things aren't going so well with her and your dad?" Alexis guessed.

Sierra fidgeted with her phone, clearly uncomfortable and on edge. "I think it's getting better. But my mom isn't really willing to try. She gets herself in a huff every time they have any kind of little disagreement. I just want her to try to get along with him. I feel like she's keeping things from getting better between them."

They all waited for her to continue. Sierra leaned her head back against the chair, eyes closed. Kate climbed out of the pool to move closer to her friend. She sat on the pool deck at the end of Sierra's chair, dripping wet. Sierra finally murmured, "I mean, she's always looking for some excuse to be mad. She expects me to smooth things over between them, and when I'm not there, it all falls apart. I'm glad they have this time to themselves to try to figure things out without me. My sister's too little to really notice everything that's going on. . . . I can't be in the middle." She cut off, her voice cracking. "I just can't." Her eyes remained closed, but it was obvious that if she opened them, she would start to cry.

Alexis and Kate looked at each other, unsure of what to do or say. Kate finally said, "Sierra, you can't deal with their issues for them. . . . It's not your fault." Alexis chewed her lip and remained silent—she didn't like to deal with emotional issues. Kate reached out to hold Sierra's hand.

Finally the silence was broken by Adam. "My folks went through something similar a few years ago." He spoke quietly. "My brothers and I were always caught in the middle, and it felt like crap."

Sierra opened her eyes to look at Adam. "Really?"

"We used to hide under the stairs while they were fighting. No one wanted to be around them after a fight, since we either became targets for criticism or had to deal with my mom moping around, which just sucked." He hoisted himself out of the pool. "We used to escape to Lex's house whenever we could, just to get away. But then something must have clicked, because after about a year things started to get better. Every day a little bit more of the tension would ease up. Now it's cool again. This will sound crass, but I have to say it: They'll either work it out, or they'll end it. Something will change."

"Yeah," Sierra agreed. "I guess that's true." She nodded. "I've gone through the trial separation, then the reconciliation, then the real separation, and now whatever this is. . . . I guess it can't get a whole lot worse than this. I just want them to get to a place where it's not a mystery every day. The uncertainty makes me crazy."

Adam was nodding, as though he knew exactly how she felt. Kate hadn't known any of this about Adam, and watching him relate to Sierra so compassionately made her start to see another side of him. "It will get better," he told Sierra again. "The bickering might not end the way you'd like it to, but it *will* end."

Sierra smiled at him gratefully, then said, "You know what? There's really no point in me worrying about this here. For once I can't do anything about it, so let's just enjoy ourselves. Here we are, uninvited guests at this gorgeous pool, and I'm moaning about my parents' issues. Kate, can you teach me a double flip?"

Kate nodded, happy to see her friend in a better place. She knew Sierra was still dwelling on her conversation with her mom, but felt like the best thing they could do was help her forget about everything for a while. So they all practiced backflips and spins and cannonballs, enjoying the privacy and relaxation of the pool. At one point Adam raided the concession stand, grabbing candy bars for each of them. When he handed Kate her favorite—a 3 Musketeers—she jokingly shot him a scolding look. He grinned, then pulled four soaking-wet dollar bills out of his pocket and left them under the counter as payment for their snack.

It was near eleven when they finally decided they'd better get moving to find a place to crash for the night. Kate slipped back into the cabana to trade Adam's wet T-shirt for her jeans and tank top, and they all sat on the chairs to dry off for a few minutes.

Suddenly a loud voice boomed out, "Who's in there?"

Kate and Sierra screamed, startled and scared of getting caught. They all jumped up, and Sierra quickly pulled the lifeguard rescue ladder from its stand against the wall. Together she and Adam propped it up against the fence.

Adam scaled the ladder first, and flung his leg over the top to drop down to safety on the outside of the country club wall. The girls could hear a ring of keys rattling in the lock on the fence, and they hustled to follow Adam up and over the ladder. They had to jump from the top of the fence down into the grass on the other side of the wall, but Adam stood on the ground, ready to help catch each of them. Just as one of Kate's legs flung over the top of the fence, the door of the pool popped open and a security guard came barging in. He and Kate locked eyes for one brief moment before she flipped her other leg up and over and dropped to the ground.

As Kate scrambled to her feet on the safe side of the fence, she heard the guard call out, "You better hit the road, girls." All four of them went running, wet, happy, and a tiny bit freaked out, back to the safety of their car.

A few minutes later they were back on the road again.

Six

Michigan

"How do my boobs look?" Alexis adjusted her shirt so it was barely covering the top edges of her bra. Her tiny chest had been squished into a push-up bra that made her A cups look like a solid B-C, and every little bit was spilling out of the top of her shirt.

"Pretty impressive," Sierra replied. "If you're not careful, those suckers are going to take that last step right out of your shirt and walk to the party themselves."

Kate laughed. "She's right, Lex. Your boobs are pushed up about as far as they can be without actually removing them from your body. Great shirt. I'm sure Kevin will be glad to see them . . . uh, you."

"Funny," Alexis said dryly. "Geez, you

guys. I'm so nervous!" She giggled, then covered her mouth with her hand. "I don't know why I'm being such a ditz. You would think the nerves would disappear after two years together, but I swear . . . I'm panicking at the thought of seeing him."

Kate squeezed her friend's hand, but stayed silent. She was just as nervous as Alexis about this reunion with Kevin. A surprise visit to a total cad of a boyfriend just wasn't a good idea, and Kate was paranoid about what they were going to find. She really wanted to support Alexis's relationship but just couldn't. Much as she wanted to believe in true love, Kate had a hard time understanding Alexis's romance with Kevin. She just didn't get it—but watching Alexis prepare for her reunion all day had made Kate even more excited about the fact that they were only a day away from Love!

They had spent the night before at a seedy roadside motel very near the country club. It had been late when they'd left the pool, and Adam had wanted to sleep on a real mattress so he'd be rested for his interview the next day. The motel was only an hour from the university, so they had slept in and then had driven to Ann Arbor around lunchtime to check out the campus and check into their hotel. Since they'd gone cheap the previous night, they decided to splurge and stay at a hotel with an indoor corridor, rather than a place where you could drive up to your room door.

Alexis had called Kevin at work that morning, but hadn't told him they were in town. She was determined to surprise him. He had mentioned the fact that his fraternity was hosting a party that night. So the three girls were on their way there now, with Alexis's boobs leading the way. Adam had spent the afternoon at his interview, and was now having dinner with a student on the scholarship committee. He was planning to meet up with them later at the frat house.

"Kat, can you figure out where we're going?" Alexis had stopped and was scanning addresses for the right frat house. Lex had never been to visit Kevin before, and was struggling to reconcile the setting Kevin had described over the phone with the real-life college block they were wandering down now.

"It's right there, Alexis," Kate responded, pointing at the big brick building directly in front of them. "Are you ready?" Kate adjusted her own shirt, pulling uncomfortably at the stretchy, shimmery green material in the humid heat. She noticed Sierra was doing the same thing, and Kate smiled to herself.

Alexis had insisted upon outfitting them all for the party, which meant Kate and Sierra were both uncomfortably stuffed into shirts borrowed from Alexis's suitcase. Kate's was far tighter than she would usually wear, and she felt like she was squeezed inside a roll of duct tape. The electric blue strapless shirt Sierra was wearing was a few inches too short for her long frame, but pulling it down to cover her belly risked a full-frontal boob flash. Sierra squirmed to try to shrink herself to fit into it.

There was a mob of people on the porch outside the frat house, several of whom looked drunk already. As the three girls made their way up the steps toward the front door, a scrawny guy shouted out a second-floor window. "Caitlin!" He was waving at Sierra out the window, so she timidly waved back.

She crinkled her forehead at Alexis and Kate. "Who is that guy?"

They shrugged, and proceeded into the

house. Inside, the living room—if you could call it that—was packed. It was humid and hot, and the music was so loud they couldn't hear their own voices. Alexis led them through the room, scanning for Kevin in the crowd. He was nowhere to be found on the main floor, but Alexis found herself stalked by potential suitors as she made her way through the kitchen and den. She was constantly cut off by guys who looked first at her chest, then at her face, and usually said something along the lines of, "Where have you been all my life?"

Alexis seemed flattered at first, but quickly bored of the cheesy line. "Kevin chose *this* over *me* this summer?" she mused, flipping her hair over her shoulder. Sierra shrugged, clearly unimpressed by the party.

Kate's left butt cheek was squeezed as they made their way upstairs, but when she turned around to see who it was, all she saw was a guy and girl making out a few steps below her. Sierra's window friend appeared out of nowhere when they got to the second floor. He wrapped Sierra in a big hug and said, "I was hoping you'd come!"

"Babe, I think you're mistaking me for

someone else," Sierra said gently, prying the guy's hands off her back.

"Get lost, loser," Alexis said with more force. When the guy just stood there staring, she said, "Seriously, freak. You don't know her."

"Lex," Kate cautioned. "Be nice. He's just confused."

"He's drunk," Alexis said. "So he's acting stupid. I don't want him to touch my friend and use booze as his excuse. It's vile."

The guy chuckled, then wandered off down the hall. He yelled back, "I'll find you later, Caitlin. We have catching up to do." He blew a kiss at Sierra, and they all burst out laughing. The guy laughed too, confident that he was in on the joke.

"Ick." Kate shuddered. "Creepy."

They peeked into each of the rooms on the second floor, but found no sign of Kevin anywhere. A group was playing Twister in one room, and Alexis knocked one guy down when she shoved the door open. "Oops." She looked amused rather than apologetic. Continuing their climb up to the third floor, Alexis said, "What if he's not here yet?"

"Then we'll wait for him," Sierra promised. "We can dance and hang out. We're meeting Adam here, anyway, so we have time to kill."

The third floor was quieter than the lower levels, and each of the rooms they peeked into were either empty or had small clusters of people who were listening to music and chilling. The door at the far end of the hall was open, and they could hear John Mayer playing inside. Kate peeked in, and what she saw made her close the door quickly behind her. "Nothing in there," she said cheerfully, her voice squeaky and high.

Alexis whitened. "You're clearly lying, Kate. You always do that high voice thing when you're lying. Is Kevin in there?" She looked nervous.

As she should, Kate thought. Kevin was, in fact, inside—and he wasn't alone. "No," Kate lied, flashing a desperate look at Sierra. Her voice went up another octave and she sounded overly excited. "We should go back downstairs. I'm thirsty."

Alexis pushed past Kate and opened the door. Kate and Sierra followed apprehensively. Kevin was sitting on a beanbag chair, with a girl who looked eerily similar to Alexis perched squarely on his lap. The girl's head was resting on his shoulder, and his hand was cupped around her knee. They both looked up, and Kevin's face caught on faster than his hand did. The shock was evident in his expression, and finally he released his hand from the girl's knee. He pushed her off of himself and jumped up.

"Surprise," Alexis muttered, her eyes narrowing.

"Lex!" Kevin cried. "What are you doing here?"

"It's good to see you, too, asshole."

"Lex, she's not . . ." He looked at the girl who'd been on his lap and who was now standing there staring at Kevin with her hands on her hips. "We're just . . ." He lowered his voice to a whisper. "I can't get her away from me. She's totally nuts. I mean, psycho, and she thinks she has a chance with me."

Alexis smiled at Kevin. "Oh, isn't that an unfortunate problem. You're being so sweet to let her play out her little fantasy. *On. Your. Lap.*" Alexis was acting tough, but Kate knew her friend was hurt. On Kate's right Sierra crossed her arms and stepped up to show she had Alexis's back.

"Lex, don't act like that," Kevin pleaded. "I'm so glad you're here." He moved to hug her. "Why *are* you here?" Alexis shrugged him off.

"I came to see *you*, you lying, disgusting pig. Now I've seen you, and I don't need to again." Alexis turned and walked out of the room.

Kate and Sierra turned to follow her. Kevin grabbed Kate's arm as she stepped into the hall, and he said, "She's really mad, isn't she? Will you let me explain?"

Kate looked at him in disbelief. "Kevin, I think you got off pretty easy. You're a jerk—you always have been, and always will be—and she should have done a lot more than just walk out of here. I'm surprised you're not in physical pain. If you ever try to call her again, I'll find you and make sure that you regret treating Alexis like this. Got it?" She delivered this message with a big sugary smile, then hurried off to find her friends. Her blood was boiling and her hands were visibly shaking. Alexis didn't deserve to be treated like this, and—even though she had sort of seen it coming—Kate hadn't thought Kevin could be so completely disrespectful of their relationship.

If Lucas ever did that to me . . . , Kate thought somberly as they climbed back down the stairs. But she knew Lucas would *never* do that.

Back downstairs Alexis yelled through the noise, "I guess I can't say I'm surprised." She looked more angry than hurt. "When he told me he wasn't coming home at all this summer, I guess I sort of knew we were close to the end." She shook her head. "I didn't really prepare myself to actually *see* him with someone else, so that really sucks. Man, this is so embarrassing." She chewed her lip.

"Lex." Kate reached out to pull her friend into a hug. "Lex, you guys have been together for two years. You don't have to be embarrassed about feeling sad."

Alexis blew her bangs away from her face and blinked a few times to compose herself. "No, he's an asshole, and I don't want to waste any more time on him by feeling crappy about our relationship fizzling out."

Kate couldn't stop herself from smiling. She and Alexis were such opposites—Kate couldn't help but think about how she would have felt if that *had* been her with Lucas. She knew that she and Alexis processed things differently. It would have taken Kate at least a year to recover; she suspected Lex would be mostly recovered by later that night. "If it makes you feel better," Kate yelled over the music, "I will remove his toenails one by one if he ever calls you or in any way hurts you again." Sierra nodded her agreement.

"Oh, Kat." Alexis smiled. "My hero. Grrrrrr . . . ," she growled. "If you girls don't mind, I see no reason to waste this Wonderbra. Excuse me." She air-kissed at them, then sauntered over to a hot guy who had been eyeing her from across the room. Sierra and Kate watched as Alexis expertly flirted with him, laughing and chatting as though nothing had happened that night to put her off her game.

"How does she *do* that?" Sierra wondered aloud.

Kate shrugged. "That's Lex, right?"

"I'm actually sort of jealous. How long did it take me to stop mourning my breakup with James last winter? Like, four months?"

"Something like that. You were miserable! I'm sure Lex is pretty broken up too, but she's so good at distracting herself." Kate pursed her lips, remembering Sierra's breakup with the guy she'd gone out with for a few months at the beginning of the year. "If it were me . . ."

"Let's not even go there," Sierra said, and shook her head. "I really have to pee," she declared. "Look, there's Adam." She pointed toward the front door, then said, "Will you be okay if I go look for a toilet?" Kate didn't say anything, but Sierra grinned and said, "Oh, of course you'll be okay. . . You and Adam will be just fine."

Kate called after Sierra, "Hey, what does that mean?" Sierra just smiled and headed off into the crowd. Kate waved at Adam—he looked so different with his hair all tidy and his shirt tucked in. He'd bought a blue and white striped button-down for the interview, and it still had some of the crisp creases from being folded into its package. Kate couldn't help but giggle when she saw how straight-laced he looked, considering his usual tousled hair and T-shirt style.

"How'd it go?" she shouted over the music.

Adam gave her a thumbs-up and looked around the crowded room. "Is Lex off with Kevin?"

"Um, no," Kate shouted back. She pointed toward the front door and said, "Let's go outside and I'll fill you in." They headed out onto the porch, which was emptier than it had been when they'd arrived. The keg had been set up down in the basement, and most people had migrated down there to be closer to it.

They sat on the front steps, and Kate recounted the events of Alexis and Kevin's reunion. She also told Adam that Alexis was now off exacting her revenge on Kevin with one of his frat brothers.

"Oof, that's brutal," Adam declared. "I've always hated Kevin, so good for her."

"Really? You hated Kevin?" Kate asked. She'd figured Adam hadn't ever really thought about it or cared about his cousin's relationship, but maybe he had.

"Didn't *you*? He never treated Alexis right." Adam grabbed a soda out of the cooler on the porch next to him. "Want one?"

"Oh, sure. Can I get a Cherry Coke?"

"Not a diet?" Adam asked.

"What's that supposed to mean?"

"Nothing. It's just that girls always take diet soda."

"I don't."

"I guess not. That's cool." Adam clicked his can against Kate's in a little toast. "You're cool, Kate."

Kate furrowed her forehead. *Is he being serious, or rude?* Kate couldn't read Adam, and it bugged her. "Why do you say that?"

"I like that you say what you want, and it's fun when you fight back." Adam tipped back his soda, offering no further explanation.

"It's fun when I fight back?"

"Sure. That's why I like hanging out with you—you're a challenge. Don't you get a rush when we fight?"

Is he serious? Kate wondered. "Not really," she answered, partially lying. "I don't understand why you have to be such a jerk all the time," she said truthfully.

Adam laughed. "Come on, now. I'm not a jerk. You just don't see my side of the argument. I can't be that bad. You liked me when we were kids."

"You're a total asshole now, though," Kate declared. "You turned evil in sixth grade, when you spread that rumor about Alexis sleeping with Barbie dolls. It took her months to live that down."

"*That's* why you hate me?" Adam asked. "Because I told people about my cousin's Barbie doll fascination?" He looked surprised, then amused. "That was a true story, you know."

"Whatever." Kate dismissed him with her hand. "It was a crappy thing to do, and I don't like when people don't treat my friends with respect."

Adam was grinning. "Seriously? Your grudge against me is that I spread a rumor about my cousin in *sixth* grade? Well, aren't you a loyal friend."

"Yeah, I am. And you're not such a great cousin. You took private information that you had only because you're family and turned it into a rumor, just to be mean to Alexis."

"Did you know . . . ," Adam started, then broke off.

Kate looked at him critically. "What? Did I know what?"

He took a swig of his soda and shook his head. "Nothing."

They sat in silence, watching people walk by the frat house. Every few minutes someone would come out the front door, looking for relief from the noise and heat inside the party. Kate heard some girls talking about the length of the line for the bathroom, so she guessed Sierra was stuck in it.

The heat of the evening was oppressive, and Kate stretched her hands up, searching for a breeze in the sticky air. When she lowered her arms, she propped them behind her on the porch so she could lean back to look up at the brilliant stars that seemed almost dull back in Jersey.

Adam followed suit, and as he placed his hands on the disintegrating wood of the porch, his hand unintentionally grazed hers. He left it where it was, his pinky finger overlapping with hers. His relaxed posture suggested the touch meant nothing, but Kate was singularly focused on his hand, and her entire body, from the tips of her ears to her purple-painted baby toe, was buzzing.

Finally Adam said quietly, "In the interest of full disclosure, I should mention that right before sixth grade Alexis told every single one of my friends that I wet the bed every time I slept over at her house. She also told them that her parents had bought a special plastic sheet with Teletubbies on it for the bed I slept on so that I wouldn't ruin the mattress." He smiled. "*That* is why I told people the very true story of Alexis and her Barbie dolls. Peeing the bed is not something to joke about. Man, I was *tortured* after she spread that story."

"Was it true?" Kate asked, laughing.

Adam sat up, causing their fingers to pop apart.

"No, it wasn't true!" Adam feigned anger, but he was laughing, too. Suddenly he said, "We used to be friends, Kate."

"I know. Stuff happens, I guess."

"I always liked hanging out with you. Remember that summer when we canoed out to the island almost every day, just you and me? That was actually the summer I started to play the banjo too, if I remember correctly."

"Yeah," Kate answered, thinking back to one of their first summers in Love, when she and Adam had spent almost every afternoon together while everyone else went waterskiing. It was before the Barbie incident, and long before Lucas's family had started coming to Cattail Cottages Resort. "You were the only other person that didn't like to spend every second on the boat. My anti-waterskiing companion."

"I actually really like waterskiing. I'm no good at it, but it's still fun."

"Why didn't you go at all that summer?"

"Because . . ." Adam turned toward her. "Because then you would have been stuck all alone or gotten roped into riding around in the boat watching everyone else ski. Chilling out with just you was always a lot more fun anyway. You've always cracked me up, princess, and I liked hanging out with you. . . . Still do."

Just then Alexis and Sierra both came barreling out the front door. Alexis was wild-eyed, and Sierra was laughing hysterically. "Let's go!" Alexis called, running down the front steps. "We have to get away from Sierra's lover."

As they all took off down the sidewalk toward their car, they could hear a guy yelling, "Caitlin, don't go! Caitlin!"

"What did you do?" Kate asked, breathing heavily as they ran down the sidewalk.

"I didn't do anything!" Sierra declared. "Lex?"

Alexis laughed harder. When they were finally in the safety of their car, back on the road to the hotel, Alexis said, "I told the drunk guy that Sierra, or rather, Caitlin, was easily wooed by poetry. So the dumb guy stripped down to his underwear and started reading random Shakespearean sonnets to her from the landing between the first and second floors. It was freaking hilarious!"

"Poor guy." Sierra laughed. "I feel bad for him."

"He was drunk, Sierra! He'll have no recollection that he did that, until someone reminds him tomorrow. Maybe he'll realize he shouldn't act like such a fool next time."

"At least he'll never see us again," Kate offered. "Even though I'm sure he'd love to see you, Caitlin." They pulled into the parking lot of their hotel. As they walked into the lobby, Kate's phone rang. "Hey," she murmured into the phone, waiting for a response on the other end. "I'm excited to see you, too." She smiled to herself, but was fully aware that her friends were watching her. "Okay, g' night." When she hung up, the other three were waiting for her next to the front desk.

"Lover boy?" Alexis asked, raising an eyebrow.

"*Yes,*" Kate said. "I can't believe I'll see him in less than a day! I just keep visualizing that moment when we'll pull up at the resort and Lucas will come greet me with a kiss. Mmmm," Kate murmured, closing her eyes to picture the scene. When she opened them again, Adam was watching her closely. "What?" she asked. "Why are you looking at me like that?"

He didn't say anything, just shook his head.

"What?" she demanded. "Are you trying to find a way to kill my fantasy, just like your cousin?" Kate looked at him angrily, anticipating the rude comment he was sure to make. "Because you won't, and your criticism will just piss me off."

"No," Adam said simply. "I'm happy for you, Kate. I hope it all unfolds exactly as it should."

Kate stared at him and realized he was being genuine. "Thank you. That's a nice thing to say." They all headed off toward the elevator to go to their shared room, but as they passed the breakfast area off the lobby, someone singsonged, "Hello, girls!"

Inside the dining room were a bunch of white-haired women, smiling and waving. "Oh, hi!" Kate said, stepping into the room. "You were at the amusement park yesterday, right? What are you doing here?"

"This is the next stop on our tour," one of the women said. "Lovely Ann Arbor. We move on to Chicago tomorrow. Then we'll be making our way up into Wisconsin and the shores of the Great Lakes!"

Another woman shouted out, "If I have

anything to say about it, we're staying in Chicago until this money in my pocket is gone! I have some shopping to do." All the other ladies laughed, despite the fact that her comment wasn't funny. Inside joke, apparently.

"Okay . . ." Alexis was obviously eager to get out of there. "Well, have a good trip. Really nice to see you again." She yawned and gestured toward the elevator.

As they were on their way out the door, one of the women said, "Do any of you kids play pinochle? Joyce went to bed, and Fern is missing her partner." A woman—presumably Fern—waved at them.

"Yeah, sure, I play. Are you willing to play with a guy, or is this ladies-only?" Adam asked, and stepped into the room.

Fern stood up and shimmied a little, then said to the other women in the room, "Ooh-hoo, girls. Look at my luck! Of course I'll play with a fellow. I've been on a bus tour with forty women for the last week and could use a little distraction!" She laughed, and Adam turned to look at Kate, who was struggling to keep from cracking up.

Adam wrapped his hand around Kate's forearm, then announced, "I'll only play if

Kate agrees to stay and help me. What do you say, Kate?" Kate looked at Adam like he was crazy, then back at the roomful of women. They were all looking up at her hopefully, so she nodded.

Alexis and Sierra both giggled behind her before saying good luck and good night. Alexis whispered, "Sorry to ditch you, but . . . Well, I'm not sorry!" Then they hustled off down the hall toward the elevator. Kate knew Alexis and Sierra would settle into one of the beds while she and Adam were downstairs, meaning she would have to fight Adam for the roll-away.

As they made their way over to Fern's table, Kate whispered, "Why are you doing this to me?"

"It will be fun," Adam whispered back. "It's quality together time for you, me, and the Q-tip tour."

"Q-tip tour?"

"Sure," Adam said, and grinned. "When they're all sitting in the bus with their white hair peeking up over the windowsills, it looks like a bunch of Q-tips lined up in a row. So it's a Q-tip tour."

"Superfunny," Kate deadpanned. They sat at Fern's table and Adam picked up the hand of cards that had been dealt to him. For the next hour Kate watched as Adam charmed and flirted with the ladies on the Q-tip tour. She had to admit that she was impressed at how friendly and charming he could be.

But more than anything, Kate was surprised at how much fun she was having. Not only were the women hilarious, but she was having a great time with Adam. It was as though they were back in the fifth grade again, having a great time hanging out—and getting along.

At one point, after proudly laying down the ace of hearts, Fern looked up at Kate and Adam. Adam was whispering something to Kate, and Fern said, "You two sure do make a charming couple." She pointed at Kate. "You're a lucky girl."

"Oh, no—," Kate said, starting to explain that they were very much not a couple.

Adam cut her off to say, "Thanks, Fern."

Before Kate could protest, the buzz of a text message in her pocket distracted her. She pulled out her cell and glanced at the screen.

The text was, of course, from Lucas,

who had simply written: "Good night, sleep tight!" Kate took that as her cue to excuse herself from the game to head off to bed. The road trip had been fun, but she couldn't wait for tomorrow to come.

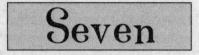 Seven

Wisconsin

"Ah, nothing says home like the smell of rotting fish carcasses." Adam rolled his window down as they passed the turtle pond that was just down the road from Cattail Cottages Resort. No one knew why it was known as the turtle pond, because in all the years they'd been coming to Love, the turtle pond had been nothing more than a boglike hole filled with mud that smelled like dead fish. Adam sniffed deeply, then coughed out, "You gotta love Love."

They had just run into Sierra's mom, who was out for a walk, and had dropped Sierra off to walk the few miles back to the resort with her. A few minutes later Alexis steered the car into the dirt parking lot at the end of the gravel road. They had been driving since very early that morning. They'd been eager to get there—Kate especially—so they'd just driven straight through with only a few quick bathroom breaks.

Alexis hopped out of the car and jogged over to the main house to grab a wagon they could use to pull their stuff from the car to their cabins. Lucas was nowhere nearby, so Kate started to unload the bags, eager to get to her cabin, where he'd surely be waiting.

Adam came up behind Kate and reached around her to get his arm into the trunk. "Can I help?" he murmured, gently pulling her hand off Alexis's huge suitcase. His hand stayed on hers for what felt like a few seconds longer than necessary, and while his skin touched hers, Kate's heart stood still. Her chest constricted, catching her breath between her ribs and holding it hostage there.

"Thanks," she muttered when finally he pulled his hand and the bag back out of the trunk. *I guess I'm extra sensitive now that I'm finally so close to Lucas*, she reasoned.

Adam smiled his dopey grin at her, and walked away from the car. She shook the flirty sensation off and grabbed her duffel bag out of the trunk. When they had everything loaded up in the giant wagon, the three of them headed off toward the cabins near the lake.

Their families always rented the same cottages, so instinct led them each toward their usual summer homes. Kate's family was in cabin four, Alexis's was in two, and Adam's family rented cabin number seven, which was sort of off by itself around a curve on the lakeshore. Lucas's family rented one of the more distant cabins with greater privacy and better views of the lake. As they approached Kate's and Alexis's cabins, Adam grabbed his bag off the wagon and said, unceremoniously, "See you later. Thanks for the lift."

Kate and Alexis split up a moment later, agreeing to meet before the bonfire that night. For as long as they could remember, every night there was a group barbecue, followed by a bonfire where all the under-twenties hung out until the mosquitoes got too persistent for anyone to stay outside any longer. The trick, Kate had learned, was to sit in the line of the campfire smoke, and the mosquitoes stayed away. That was her plan for that night, when she wanted to stretch her first evening with Lucas out until the last possible moment.

Kate stepped inside her family's cabin, and was happy to see that nothing had changed from the summer before. There was a lumpy futon couch that divided the kitchenette from the living room. She and her sister fought every year over who got to sleep in the tiny second bedroom, and which of them was relegated to the futon in the common room. The "dining area" was defined by a warped card table that stood between the other side of the kitchenette and the bathroom. The table still had a small hole where Kate and Alexis had dropped a burning candle during a late-night giggle fest more than five years before.

As Kate surveyed her surroundings, the screen door burst open and her little sister, Gina, came charging in. "Oh." Gina stopped short when she saw Kate. "You're here. Mom! Kate's here!"

"Hey, G," Kate replied, and smiled at her sister. Gina was fourteen—and the boss of the family. Gina had been a competitive figure skater since she was four, and the whole family revolved around Gina's skating practices, competitions, and performances. Kate had never excelled at anything, so she just tried to stay out of the way while everyone planned around Gina. "When did you guys get here?"

"Two days ago," Gina replied, while applying a shiny lacquer to her lips. "You're on the futon."

Kate rolled her eyes. "Whatever." She would deal. It was easier to just relent than to fight with Gina, who would surely find a means to get her way. Kate planned to spend most of the summer with Lucas, anyway, so it's not like she'd be hanging out in her room reading books or anything.

"Have you seen Lucas yet?" Gina asked, innocently enough.

"No. We just got here," Kate responded as evenly as she could. "Why? Have you?"

Gina giggled. "He's cute, Kate. Cuter than last year. And he's been talking about you." Gina was a romantic, just like her sister, and she knew all about Kate's kiss from last summer. Even though Kate and her sister weren't all that close, Kate enjoyed talking to her about guys. Gina *got* guys.

"Really?" Kate's anticipation bubbled up inside, and she could hardly stop herself from running out of the cabin and straight into Lucas's arms.

"But he's out on the boat." Gina frowned dramatically. "He and some of the other guys went out waterskiing about an hour ago. If it's like yesterday, they probably won't be back until it gets dark. Well . . . see ya! I'll send Mom inside in a little bit to help you with your sunscreen. You need it, whitey." Gina spun and flounced back out the door to go back down to the dock.

They won't be back until dark? Kate mused. It seemed her Lucas reunion would have to wait . . . but Kate didn't know if she could stand the suspense.

Kate brushed her teeth for the third time in half an hour, carefully stretching the bristles to reach the way back teeth. After she rinsed, she rolled her tongue in her mouth, checking for any residual Cheetos film. All clear.

She trotted back out to the living room and grabbed her jeans. The cool evening buzzing with abundant mosquitoes and sand flies made long pants a wise choice. Kate was pleased, since she'd always felt her legs had never looked quite right in shorts. She had one of those better-naked sorts of bodies. Long pants were okay, but there was something about the way shorts cut her thighs in two that just didn't work. She'd tried the long shorts style, but then her calves looked stumpy.

Kate was okay with her body, but struggled to find the right way to outfit it. She'd always wanted to be a skirt person, but her family didn't have the right income to support a multifaceted wardrobe for Kate *and* a skating career for Gina. Kate could wear the same jeans most days and no one noticed or cared. But she worried it would be pretty obvious if she started wearing the same decorative skirt every Tuesday and Thursday. So she just stuck with her basic style.

She spun around, studying her reflection in the big picture window at the front of the cabin. It was getting dark out, and the light inside caused the window to function more like a mirror. She knew that people rarely used the hidden path that ran past the cottage, so she didn't worry that anyone would see her checking herself out. She pulled her tank top on over her head, tugged it into place, and then promptly pulled it back off again. Too bland for her Lucas reunion.

A rejected green T-shirt, brown wrap top, and black halter later, Kate was still only half-dressed. A knock at the door startled her out of her clothing-induced frenzy. "Alexis, thank god," Kate declared when the door creaked open. (Kate had covered up with a dish towel.) "I can't find anything to wear."

Alexis brushed past Kate and started pawing through the mounds of shirts piled up on the floor. "Try this one," Alexis demanded, pulling off her own light blue cotton polo. Kate pulled Alexis's still-warm shirt over her own head. It was tight, but in the good way. "Yep." Alexis nodded. "That's the one."

"Really, Lex? You're sure?"

"Yup. I've been looking for a good excuse to steal your hot pink tank, and I think I just found it. Deal?"

"Deal. Did you see him out there when you passed the fire pit?"

"Who, Adam?" Alexis teased. Kate was annoyed at the joke. "Oh, *Lucas*? No, he's not there yet. The boat isn't at the dock, so they must still be out on the lake."

"Oh, well, that's okay." Kate pretended to be upbeat, but inside she was frustrated that Lucas hadn't been around all day to see her. He had known she was getting to Love today, and she had really hoped he would be waiting for her when she arrived. Obviously that was silly, since Lucas couldn't make his brothers and friends sit around waiting for him to go out waterskiing, but still . . .

Alexis could sense Kate's frustration and reached out to touch her arm. "It's not really okay," Alexis verified. "He should have been around when we got here. You've been waiting all year."

Just then the whir of the speedboat motor cut through the quiet evening, and they could hear guys' voices down on the dock. Sierra came bursting into Kate's cabin, out of breath. "Lucas is back!" Her dramatic flair made Alexis start laughing hysterically, while Kate paced in semi-freak-out mode. She'd been waiting so long for this moment, and it was finally here.

"So? Are you going to go grab him and make out?" Alexis nudged Kate toward the door. "Go on. Get your guy."

Kate stepped out onto the cabin's tiny front porch and made her way down the gravel path that led to the lake. She wanted her reunion with Lucas to be perfect and knew she had to be alone—so her friends hung back.

Her family's cabin was close to the resort's main beach and the docks, but the resort's barbecue area stood between her and the lake. There was a huge group gathered near the barbecues, eating hot dogs and bratwurst. Kate's parents stood chatting with Adam's. Sierra's parents cuddled together on a log bench, apparently getting along. Gina and Sierra's little sister, Sasha, were giggling about something while Jake, one of the guys who worked at the resort, was working on getting the bonfire going. A group of guys hung around near Jake, tossing sticks into the fire. Kate tried to step past everyone to hurry down to the lake. Just when she thought she was in the clear, Adam stepped out of the group of guys and grabbed her arm to stop her.

"Let go." Kate twisted away.

Adam looked startled. "Sorry," he snapped back. "I just wanted to say hey. I got used to seeing you all day."

"Oh." Kate chewed her lip, feeling guilty for being snippy. She could see some of the guys unloading their gear from the boat onto the dock, and Kate knew she needed to hurry if she was going to catch Lucas before he made his way up the hill to his family's cottage. "I have to go," she said bluntly.

She turned away from Adam, and stopped

short when she came face-to-face with the one she'd been dreaming about all year: green eyes, sandy blond hair, chiseled cheekbones— a perfect specimen of summer boy. "Adam," she said, her smile cutting across her face. Then she realized what she'd said, and hastily corrected herself. "*Lucas*. Lucas . . . hi."

"Hi, Kate." Lucas was holding two wet life jackets. He handed them to Adam— who was standing right behind her—so he could pull Kate into a hug. "It's great to see you," he murmured into her ear.

All of Kate's senses were buzzing. Everything felt right as she pressed against him, his bare chest separated from hers by only a tiny bit of shirt fabric. The hug lasted only a few seconds, but in those moments she could feel his breath rising and falling. The droplets of lake water in his hair ran down his neck and onto Kate's cheek, which was pressed against his bare shoulder. The world around them faded away, and Kate could only feel the sensation of his body against hers.

"You look good. I missed your hot body," Lucas said as he pulled away, which made Kate happy about her shirt choice, even if the body comment was a little bit crass.

"Wow." Adam was still standing next to them, and he started clapping his hand against one of the life jackets. "That's romantic, man."

"What?" Lucas said, draping an arm around Kate's shoulder. She melted into the warmth of his embrace, looking forward to time alone with him later. Alone—and away from Adam.

"Nothing. Carry on, Prince Charming." He laughed obnoxiously, then passed the wet life jackets back to Lucas.

Kate spat out, "It's fitting that you would comment on someone else's charm, Adam." Then she grabbed Lucas's available arm and pulled him toward the fire pit. There was no way Adam was going to ruin the romantic reunion Kate had been planning all year. No way. Even though he was sort of right.

She noticed that Adam was still watching them when she settled in next to Lucas on an empty log bench near the bonfire. Kate closed her eyes, desperate to get Adam's face out of her mind. When she did, Lucas took it as his cue to pick things up where they'd left off last summer.

He leaned in and touched her cheek,

his lips close to hers. Startled that things were playing out the way she'd imagined them, Kate's eyes snapped open, and the moment was lost. She closed them again, eager to recapture the moment, but nothing happened. When she cracked her lids open, Lucas was smiling at her and his face sparkled mischievously. "We have time," he whispered, his hand cradling the back of her neck. "Let's take this slow."

Kate nuzzled against him as the sun dipped lower in the sky. He wrapped his big zip-up sweatshirt around her, and the rest of the world just melted away.

Eight

In Love, Wisconsin

When Kate woke up the next morning, she was still wrapped in Lucas's sweatshirt, her body tucked up against one edge of the futon. She had forgotten to take his shirt off after the bonfire, and when she'd gotten back to her cabin, she'd decided to wear it to bed. She held it up to her face and breathed in Lucas's familiar scent.

"Are you smelling your boyfriend's sweatshirt?" Gina had just dragged herself into the living room, and was pouring a cup of coffee in the kitchenette right next to Kate's bed. Their parents had already snuck out for their morning walk, so the girls were alone in the cabin. "Had fun last night?

"Are you drinking coffee?" Kate stuffed

Lucas's sweatshirt under her and rolled onto her stomach, watching as Gina sipped coffee while she made herself a bowl of instant oatmeal for breakfast. "Yeah, I had a good night."

"Was the big reunion as perfect as you'd imagined it?" Gina was using a mocking voice, but Kate knew she wanted the dirt.

"It was good," Kate admitted. "You were right—he is cuter than last year!"

"And sweet, too. He sent you home with a sweatshirt. A real gentleman. What are you guys going to do today?"

"Dunno." Kate stepped out of bed and sat at the folding table, watching Gina flutter around the kitchen. "We're meeting up this morning. I guess I should get dressed and head down to the dock."

"You could use a little color before he sees you in your suit," Gina said, and slurped up her last bite of oatmeal. "You look pasty."

Kate rolled her eyes. "Wow. Thanks, G."

"Make sure you shave your legs too. I can see the stubblies from here." She giggled, then traipsed off to the bedroom to change into her suit.

After scarfing down a couple of pieces

of toast, Kate brushed her teeth. She hastily shaved her legs in the tiny bathroom pedestal sink, then slipped on her suit and sunscreen. The suit was a one-piece, but the cut of the legs was slightly more revealing than her previous years' suits. The pale blue color worked well with her hair, making it look close to blond, and when her hair was braided into two loose braids down either side of her neck—as it usually was—she was pretty confident she looked cute. She threw a pair of thin sweats on over her suit and made her way out to the dock.

Sierra was already at the lake, soaking in the sun with her sister. Sierra's sister, Sasha, was painfully shy, so when Kate showed up with her folding chair, Sasha went off to walk along the sandy shoreline alone.

"So? How was the kiss?" Sierra demanded as soon as they were alone. She had returned to her cabin early the night before, long before Kate and Lucas had called it a night.

Kate frowned. "No kiss yet. I'm sure he's waiting until we're alone. He's being a gentleman, right?"

"If that's how you see it," Sierra teased, lifting her eyebrows.

Just then Lucas and his brother arrived.

"Morning, ladies!" Lucas called. "How was your sleep, Kate?"

Kate blushed, realizing this was the first time she'd seen Lucas in the daylight. His shirt was off again, and she wanted to jump up and rub her hands against his tan skin. It looked so warm and soft, and she knew it felt amazing when he pressed against her. But she knew she had to wait until later, when they could be alone for real. "I slept well," she answered calmly.

"You're coming out on the boat with us today, right, Kate?"

"Oh," Kate said, realizing that meant they would be spending their first day together on the boat with all the guys. "Sure, that sounds fun."

Sierra looked at her quizzically, knowing Kate had never liked waterskiing—it just wasn't her idea of fun. And Kate hated hanging out on the boat while everyone else was waterskiing. She always had. It made her feel like some sort of pitiful groupie, just sitting in the boat watching everyone else ski. Sierra also knew Kate had been hoping for some alone time with Lucas, and the boat wouldn't be the place they could get that.

"Cool," Lucas said. "Let me grab you a

life jacket, and we can take off. Sierra, you want to come?"

"I'm happy here," Sierra answered.

"Your loss," Lucas's brother, Zack, said while hauling gear from the little storage cabin under the boat up to the main deck. "Lucas and I set up a killer course yesterday. You could see us in action."

"Whee, fun," Kate muttered under her breath, loud enough for only Sierra to hear. She grinned at her friend, then stood up to step into the boat. "Hopefully I'll be back soon. . . . Like, twenty minutes?"

"Don't count on it," Sierra teased.

Lucas revved the motor on the boat, signaling his readiness to leave. He held his hand out to Kate, and she stepped into the boat, fastening her life jacket. Lucas patted the seat that backed up against his. With her there, he could keep one of his hands on the wheel and another around her shoulder, which is exactly the scenario she would have set up if she had orchestrated the whole thing herself.

Kate beamed, excited that Lucas had invited her to join them, despite the fact that she never had enjoyed this exact activity. She felt special somehow, invited to be part of his day. It seemed like he wanted to integrate her into his summer, and she was willing to hang out on the boat with him if it meant they could talk and snuggle.

But about an hour later, after they'd picked up some of the other waterskiing crew from their cabins across the lake, Kate and Lucas had yet to exchange more than just a few words at a time. The roar of the boat was overwhelming, and there wasn't a lot of opportunity to talk. There had also been absolutely no cuddling, beyond an arm draped casually across the back of her seat. For the most part Lucas was engrossed in driving the boat and making sure they got people up on their skis and safely back into the boat. The other guys mostly ignored her.

The scene reminded her of one of those movies where the guys do very manly stuff, like fight gladiators and race cars, and the poor women are stuck sitting on the sidelines watching and cheering and eating cake or doing some other useless activity. But in Kate's scene the guys were all waterskiing and she was stuck watching and shivering and pretending to have fun from her seat in the boat. She felt like a total outsider. It wasn't fun to sit there like a limp fish just watching. She would much rather have been doing her own thing while Lucas was water-skiing, then have gotten some time alone with him later to catch up.

Right when she had resolved to tell him just that, Lucas turned around in his seat to say, "Have you ever skied? Want to try?"

"Um, yeah," Kate said, answering his first question. "I skied a few times when I was younger, but I seriously lack coordination. It's just not my thing."

"That's cool," he said, nodding and turning back to look at the open lake in front of him.

"So, um, what else do you like to do?" Kate had to shout this over the roar of the boat motor. The question embarrassed her, but it had slipped out before she had been able to think about it. It sounded like she knew nothing about him, which wasn't true, but she realized they'd never really talked about anything outside their summer world.

She only vaguely knew about his life beyond Love from his e-mails and texts over the past year. She knew he played hockey, and she knew he'd been up for homecoming king (but hadn't won), and that he was going to be a freshman at Notre Dame in the fall, but other than that, he was sort of a mystery. She wanted to know simple things, such as what he liked to do for fun on a regular day.

"What?" Lucas yelled over the roar of the motor.

"Nothing," Kate said, happy to have the opportunity to retract her stupid question.

"You look good with your hair all wild like that," Lucas said, and grinned. He twisted a strand of hair that had been blown free from her braids around his finger. "It's nice having you on the boat with me. You sure you don't want to try waterskiing again?"

Kate shook her head. "I'll try just about anything else, but not that."

"Okay. I don't want you to get hurt or anything, anyway," Lucas said seriously. "You can just sit there and look gorgeous." He held her cheek in his palm and grinned.

Kate gritted her teeth when she realized he wasn't kidding. Now she felt even more useless, and felt like a total doormat of a girl to boot—what a waste of time. Just sit there and look pretty. Ugh.

It was sweet that he'd called her gorgeous, but she could take care of herself, and didn't need him to protect her. Now she was sort of tempted to go skiing, just to show him she could handle herself just fine in the water *and* look good afterward, thankyouverymuch.

But since she truly didn't *want* to water-ski, she decided it was far more respectable to go back to the dock and hang out with her friends while Lucas got the skiing out of his system. Then they could get some quality together time later—when they could really talk and build their relationship. So the next time he slowed the boat down to switch skiers in the water, Kate said, "Lucas, would you mind taking me back to the resort? Maybe we can hang out later?"

Lucas obliged, and steered the boat back toward the resort to drop Kate off. Now Sierra and Alexis were sitting on the dock, along with Adam and one of his brothers, Danny. Jake, who worked at the resort, was cleaning the canoes on shore and flirting with Alexis. It was pretty obvious that he was making headway—she had her head tipped back, laughing hilariously at something he had said.

When Lucas pulled the boat up to the dock, Jake strolled over to catch it and tie it up. "Hey, no worries, man," Lucas said. "We're going back out. You can leave us untied. I just needed to drop this beautiful girl off first."

Everyone on the dock was staring at Kate and Lucas as he helped her out of the boat. She stood on the driver's seat to climb onto the dock, stumbling slightly when the boat rocked in the water. Lucas, who stood beneath her, held her hand to steady her. But just as she reached her leg out to step onto the dock, he grabbed her around the middle and pulled her back down so she was standing on the seat and he was standing beneath her on the floor of the boat.

He spun her around and his green eyes shone up at her in the midday sun. Still holding her around her middle, he eased her down toward him. Lucas wrapped his arms around her and she could feel the heat from his tan arms penetrating through her own cool skin. His face was close to hers, and his upper lip curled into a smile before bringing her in for a soft, sensual kiss. Her eyes closed, and the boat spun beneath her as the kiss pierced through her body. She melted into his arms, and felt the warmth of his lips against her own.

It was the kiss she'd been waiting a year for . . . and the wait had been worth it.

"My legs feel like they weigh about three tons," Kate huffed out between steps. That afternoon she and Sierra had decided to go running—but Kate had forgotten how much she disliked it. She preferred exercises that integrated naturally into her daily life—walking, biking, swimming in the lake. Sierra's long legs propelled her easily down the gravel road, but Kate felt like she was hauling a third grader on her back.

"You're doing great," Sierra cheered. "You'll feel great later—full of energy."

"I highly doubt that," Kate grumbled good-naturedly.

Sierra laughed, checking her watch. "We can head back whenever you want. I need to turn around pretty soon anyway. My mom wants us to have family dinner tonight."

"Ooh, family dinner. That sounds promising." Kate glanced at Sierra, who had been pretty silent about the state of her parents' reconciliation since they'd gotten to the lake.

"They're trying to make it work," Sierra acknowledged. "It looked like you and Lucas were trying to make it work this morning too," she teased.

The kiss with Lucas that morning had been sensational, there was no denying that. But as soon as the moment had ended, Kate had been embarrassed that Lucas had chosen the dock as the site of their first kiss of the summer. She had felt really exposed, and would much rather have been somewhere alone with him. Her parents could have seen them, which would have mortified her no end—not to mention the fact that her dad would *not* be cool with her hooking up with someone less than a day after she'd gotten there. He didn't know the backstory, and she was pretty certain he wouldn't approve even if he did.

But still, a kiss was a kiss, and it had felt amazing. "Yeah, the kiss was great."

"Great?" Sierra asked, clearly expecting something more from Kate. "Just great?"

"It was incredible, okay?" Kate slowed down to talk. "Can we walk now?"

Sierra stopped running and reached her arms over her head to stretch. "Why are you so much less enthusiastic about the kiss *after* it happened than you were before?"

"I don't know," Kate admitted. "I guess I was just a little embarrassed that our first kiss of the year was so public, you know?"

"Public? It's not like he kissed you on the JumboTron at Yankee Stadium. . . . We were the only ones who saw it."

"I know," Kate was sweating from their run. She hoped she would cool off a little before they got back to the resort. There was nothing less flattering than blotchy post-run skin.

"Was it a little awkward because Adam was there?" Sierra was clearly trying to sound casual.

"Why would that be awkward?" Kate asked defensively.

Sierra smiled knowingly. "It just seemed like you guys were maybe starting to get along a little more at the end of the road trip. I guess I was just thinking—"

"Sierra!" Kate swatted at her friend. "That's crazy! Adam? You think I have a thing for Adam?"

"Not necessarily. Maybe it's the other way around? Maybe it's mutual?"

"Sierra! Stop."

"Okay, okay," Sierra said. "I just wanted

to check, since it seemed like there was some chemistry. But maybe not."

"Seriously, you have to stop." Kate looked at Sierra sternly. "Adam and I fought the whole road trip."

"The fighting seemed a lot like flirting."

"Okay, enough." Kate stopped walking, since they were at the outskirts of the resort and she wanted to be done with this conversation before they were within earshot of anyone else. "I'm with Lucas. You know that. I've been waiting all winter to be with him again, and now we're here and it's going to be an amazing, romantic, perfect summer. I just need some time alone with him and it will all be incredible."

Sierra grinned. "Fine."

As they approached the cabins, they could hear Alexis's laughter from near the dock. They strolled down the hill to find their friend, and when they got past the cluster of trees, they found a lot more than they'd bargained for. Alexis and Jake were lying under the big oak tree next to the lake, making out as though no one could possibly spot them.

Sierra blushed a little, then called out, "Hey, take it inside!"

Alexis just rolled away from Jake and looked up at her friends from her spot on the ground. "Hey," she purred happily. "Kat, you've met Jake, right?"

Kate nodded, then looked enviously out toward the lake, searching for Lucas's boat. With her best friend's summer romance already in full swing—mere days after the breakup with Kevin—Kate wanted Lucas to hurry up and get back from waterskiing already. This summer she finally had her chance to have the romantic ending she'd been imagining ever since she'd met Lucas, and she was ready to get on with the fairy tale already.

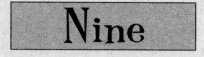Nine

Still in Love, Wisconsin

The ground was squishy between Kate's bare toes as she walked across the old football field. A storm had blown through Love the night before, washing out the evening bonfire at the resort. Kate had been stuck inside her cabin playing Yahtzee with her sister all night. Lucas and his family had gone to a friend's cabin across the lake for dinner, and the storm had forced them to stay sheltered there until late, which meant Kate and Lucas hadn't gotten the alone time she'd been looking forward to the whole day before.

Tonight, however, the air was fresh and the sky clear. The rain had washed away the humidity, so it was warm but not muggy.

Kate clutched Lucas's callused hand at her side as they made their way toward the center stage at Love's Blues Festival. The blues fest was Love's major annual celebration, and she and Lucas were going to the opening night's performances with a bunch of other kids who were staying at the resort.

Kate's shoes were off, and she was enjoying the feeling of the still-wet grass on her bare feet. The field was packed with people who had come from miles away to enjoy the weeklong festival. Kate, Lucas, Sierra, Alexis, Jake, Adam, and a few other friends from the resort had all piled into two minivans for the short drive into town. They'd parked near the ice cream shop and had walked four blocks to the other side of town and the run-down football field that held the makeshift performance stage.

"Let's sit over there," Lucas suggested, gesturing toward a rough patch of ground off to one side of the stage. He led the group across the field, holding Kate's hand tightly. After laying a blanket on the ground, Lucas pulled Kate down to sit in his lap. His hands wrapped around her waist, and his fingers tickled her bare skin between the top of her jeans and her tank top.

It was still hard for Kate to believe that she and Lucas were finally together. She'd had a crush on him for three summers, but it had always seemed like being with him would always be a fantasy rather than her reality. They'd been pretty flirty during bonfires at the end of last summer, but even then it had always been around a group, and nothing more than the one kiss had ever happened.

Kate's obsession with Lucas had initially developed because of how hot he was and—if she were being honest—how cool and unavailable he'd always seemed. She'd never imagined that they would ever move beyond the flirty stage, but their kiss at the end of last summer had changed all of that. It had been something much more than just a kiss, and Kate knew in that moment that there was potential for something much deeper.

But until their reunion a few days ago, they had never really been *together*, so it was still sort of surreal and a little unfamiliar to be with him, just hanging out as a couple. Kate had never been in a relationship before, but she'd envisioned what it would feel like her entire life. The holding hands, the sweet words whispered in her ear, the comfortable teasing between two people in love. When Kate was younger and her parents had taken her and Gina to this festival, they had watched young couples dancing and laughing and joking with friends, and she'd always been so envious. Now, finally, it was her turn, and she had the perfect boy at her side.

"Are you comfortable?" Lucas whispered in her ear, shifting his leg to help her settle in on his lap.

"Yes," Kate murmured back.

He wrapped his arms around her more snugly and pulled her in against his chest. Her heart raced—tucked against his neck, she could smell sunscreen mixed with a hint of his cologne. His body felt warm and soft against her, his arms strong and solid.

"Do you want a soda?" Adam was standing over them, pointing down at Kate. "Coke?"

Kate furrowed her brow and looked up at him, resentful of the fact that he'd crashed their moment. She knew it hadn't been intentional, though. "Um, sure, thanks."

"Lucas?"

"No, dude. I'm cool."

"You *are* cool," Adam said back, flashing a thumbs-up.

Lucas grinned, oblivious to Adam's cheeky tone. "Thanks, man. You're cool too." He held up his hand for a five. Adam responded with an unenthusiastic hand-slap, then set off with Alexis to buy sodas from the concession stand.

"Are you cold or anything?" Lucas said, rubbing Kate's arms. "Do you need my sweatshirt?"

Kate turned her head to look at his face in the darkening sky. "Lucas, it's, like, seventy degrees outside."

"So?" he said, holding her more tightly. "As your boyfriend, it's my job to make sure you're taken care of."

"Uh," Kate said, and furrowed her brow, mildly concerned about Lucas's definition of "boyfriend." (But he *had* called himself her *boyfriend*!) "I don't necessarily think that's true." She smiled at him, adjusting her position on his lap so she was still snuggled in close but better able to make eye contact.

"Oh you don't, do you?" Lucas tickled her.

"No, I don't." Kate pulled back slightly. She wanted to tell him she wasn't a damsel in distress, but realized she might come across as somewhat brusque. "It's just, I don't want you to think I'm totally helpless or anything. I'm not like that." She grinned. "I brought myself a sweater, just in case."

Lucas laughed, then whispered in her ear, "I didn't mean it like that, babe."

"Okay," Kate murmured back, then purred, "I certainly do appreciate your concern."

"Good." Lucas punctuated his response by tugging gently at her ear to turn her lips to his. She could feel him lick his lips in the instant before he leaned into her, and she could smell his spearmint gum. Her body hummed, buzzing with the anticipation of the kiss. His lips brushed hers, then pushed more persistently.

Things had just started to get interesting when Adam and Alexis returned. Adam tossed a bag of gummi worms to Sierra, who was sitting with the rest of the crew from the resort on another blanket a few feet away, then thrust a bottle of Coke toward Kate. Kate pulled back, frustrated once again by Adam's unique ability to appear everywhere he wasn't wanted exactly when he shouldn't. The road trip with the girls, her reunion with Lucas, and now, at their first real date.

He had even been there for their first kiss of the summer—gross.

Adam sat down next to Lucas, placing Kate's soda on the ground between them. "Ooh-hoo, wet ass!" He hopped up and pulled a corner of Kate and Lucas's blanket over to protect his baggy jeans from the damp grass. His tug uprooted Kate from her perch on Lucas's lap, and she tumbled off.

"Hey, watch the language around my girl," Lucas scolded jokingly. "These ears are delicate." He put his hands over Kate's ears like earmuffs.

Kate readjusted herself, now sitting right next to her boyfriend rather than *on* him. The lap thing hadn't really been working on a number of different levels. Most important, this level of PDA was a little uncomfortable. But also, she wanted to be able to see him while they chatted. She loved to look into his sharp green eyes, and think about the fact that she was the only girl who could get this close to them.

Adam snickered. "I don't think Kate really needs your protection, buddy."

"Actually," Kate said haughtily, leaning around Lucas to speak directly to Adam, "I love that Lucas is being so sweet. He treats me like a lady." She knew she sounded ridiculous saying this, and it wasn't fully true, but it pissed her off that Adam was acting like she was some sort of shrew or something.

She suddenly realized that maybe she *did* like her guy watching out for her. It wasn't as if she was a member of the X-Men, able to fight off her verbal attackers and cold weather with superhuman strength and a skintight rubber suit. She found it cute that Lucas was treating her like such a delicate flower—it was sort of a nice feeling. She figured he would soon realize how feisty she was, and this whole fairy-tale princess thing would end, but she didn't mind preserving it while it lasted. It's not like he had her locked up in a padded room or something.

"All I'm saying, Kate, is that you're pretty able to take care of yourself. If that's rude, then I'm sorry." Adam muttered the last sentence under his breath, but it was still audible.

Lucas straightened up, leaning toward Adam. "Dude, lay off." The guys were talking pretty quietly, but Kate saw Sierra get to her knees behind Adam and look over at her. Kate rolled her eyes, pretending everything was okay.

Just then the first band took the stage and the music poured over them, washing away Kate's discomfort from the little brawl that was simmering (because of her!) between Adam and Lucas. The twang of the banjo rang out across the stage as the singer took the mike. The vocalist was a surly-looking woman with a beer in one hand and a harmonica in the other. She belted out a few lyrics, and the crowd went wild.

Many people in the audience were dancing, and Alexis unabashedly joined in. She stood from her blanket and pulled Jake up to join her. Alexis reached her hand down to pull Sierra up, then came toward Kate. As Alexis approached, Kate could feel Lucas's arm seize her shoulder in something that resembled a vise grip.

Alexis leaned down to yell, "Come on, Kat!" Adam stood up to join them, but Kate stayed rooted to her spot on the blanket. She was being held down, and she looked at Lucas to figure out why he had such a strong hold on her. He was scowling at Alexis and the others, watching them suspiciously as they danced around like fools. Kate was fully jealous, and wanted to be with her friends, kicking back and having a good time.

"What do you say?" She put her mouth right up to Lucas's ear so he could hear her over the music. "Dance?"

"I wouldn't call it dancing," Lucas responded. "They're embarrassing themselves. You actually want to be a part of that?"

Kate frowned. "They're just having a good time. You don't even know anyone here. How is it embarrassing?"

"They look like losers. Besides, I can think of a better way to spend the night," he said coyly, pulling her legs over his and grabbing her into a tight hug. As the music played on, Kate melted into his embrace. She soon realized this was an easy choice . . . snuggle under the stars with her superhot boyfriend who kissed like a rock star, or dance like a nut around a broken-down stage?

Out of the corner of her eye she could see Adam slapping wildly at his knee in time with the music. Sierra was doubled over with laughter, and Alexis had her head tipped back happily—but Kate was already long gone. As the music played on, she drifted further and further away from the football field and into her own private world with Lucas.

An hour or so later the first band stepped off the stage and everyone returned to the blankets to relax and cool down. Alexis was sweating, but somehow managed to make it look sexy instead of nasty. Jake pulled her, squirming, onto his lap and tipped her back for an over-dramatic kiss. Kate turned away, embarrassed by their PDA and horrified that she'd been doing the same thing for the last hour.

Adam pulled out his banjo and strummed away, entertaining everyone in their near vicinity with his upbeat tune and goofy lyrics:

> *Well, the girl I love she's down on the dock.*
> *I love this girl, but she don't love me back.*
> *She treats me wrong, I love it bad, she's got*
>   *her hold on me.*
> *She says, Adam! You're an arrogant guy.*
> *She says, Adam! You're a pain in the ass.*
> *She treats me wrong, I love it bad, she's got*
>   *her hold on me.*
> *If she were my girl, I'd make her eggs.*
> *If she were my girl, I'd make her smile.*
> *But she treats me wrong, I love it bad, she's got*
>   *her hold on me.*

As Adam sang, Sierra sidled over, plunking down on the blanket with Kate and Lucas. Seconds later Alexis climbed off of Jake's lap and came over to sit with them as well. When Adam finished singing, he stood up and took a bow.

"So tell me, Lucas," Alexis said abruptly. "What do you usually do for fun?"

"For fun?"

Alexis nodded slowly, as though Lucas was stupid or something. "You know, with your friends?"

"We play a lot of hockey," Lucas said, and shrugged. "Hang out with the guys, stuff like that."

"Sounds fun." Alexis widened her eyes, clearly critical of Lucas's chosen pastimes. Kate was getting sick of Alexis's obvious disapproval of her boyfriend. She could be so snobby about this stuff sometimes.

Adam was sitting with them now too, and Lucas looked over and gestured to Adam's banjo. "You play the guitar, eh?"

"Yes, sir, I do—but this is a banjo." Adam grinned. "Are you a blues guy?"

"Not really," Lucas said. "I just came along tonight to hang out with my girl." He squeezed Kate's thigh. She tensed up. For some reason Lucas's hold on her was starting to feel sort of stifling.

But Alexis was watching Kate carefully, and Kate was sick of her friends judging her boyfriend. Why couldn't Alexis just be happy for her and not question Lucas's perfection? Kate smiled and leaned into Lucas, snuggling against his chest. She looked up at him and asked, "The show's good so far, don't you think?"

"It's okay," he muttered. "I've gotta get back pretty soon, though. The guys and I are going out early tomorrow, and I need to get some stuff ready down at the boat. Get some of the slalom skis in, grab a few wakeboards. Come with me?" This was more of a statement than a question, but Kate was game. Maybe some alone time, away from annoying Adam and judgmental Alexis, was exactly what they needed.

"Sure," she answered, nodding.

Lucas stood up quickly, clearly eager to go. "Grab the blanket, okay?" He picked up the cooler. "I'll take the heavy stuff." He winked, but Kate still bristled. Did he think she was a puppy?

Adam, Sierra, and Alexis were all watching Kate closely. She didn't usually take well to commands, and she knew they were waiting for her to say something that had a little bit of backbone. She didn't. Sierra picked at her fingernails, and Alexis offered them Jake's van keys to get back. But neither of them said anything more.

As Kate folded the blanket, Adam blurted out, "Gee, Kate, you must really be looking forward to trotting along behind him while he does his thing."

"What's that, dude?" Lucas clearly hadn't heard him, but Kate had. She silenced Adam with a look of pure evil, then grabbed Lucas's hand and walked away before her friends could do any more damage.

The moon was full when they returned to the resort. Kate followed Lucas down the wooded trail to the lake and his boat. She had finally shaken away the doubt that her friends had begun to plant in her mind at the blues fest, and had resolved to let Lucas take the lead. He clearly had a plan in mind, and she was a willing follower when there were kisses on the agenda.

He stepped into the boat first, then turned to help her in. The waves were echoing with *pat-pat* sounds on the edges of the dock, rocking the long fiberglass hull back and forth against the wood. Kate sat on the driver's seat while Lucas hauled skis from a storage container on the shore into the boat, then rearranged the life jackets and tow ropes in the side storage bins.

While he worked, Kate was distracted. Even though she and Lucas were finally alone in a gorgeous and romantic setting, she was having trouble concentrating on anything other than Adam. *Who does he think he is?* she wondered, wishing she could just shake his comments off. But as much as she wanted to, Kate couldn't stop caring about what Adam thought. He was like a termite, burrowing under her skin.

Finally Lucas's focus returned to Kate. He grabbed a few beach towels from the storage compartment under the front of the boat and laid them down across the open back area. She forced herself to concentrate on the scene at hand, preparing herself for what was to come.

Kate sat watching him. His arms looked extra chiseled in the shadow cast by the moonlight. "Come here." He gestured for her to join him on the floor of the boat. Then he set a firm cushion up as a backrest for her.

She snuggled into the little nest he had created, silently begging him to touch her.

On cue, his right hand slipped into hers. His left reached around her, pressing against her lower back to pull her torso in toward him. She arched slightly from the motion, and her head tilted back. Expertly Lucas swept in and brushed his lips across her neck, sending a hot current rushing through her. His lips traced slowly up her neck, stopping to pull at her ear, then making their way toward her face.

When finally his mouth reached hers, she was ready. It made her insides feel just like they had during the kiss at the end of last summer and erased all thoughts of Adam from Kate's mind like a magic wand. The questions and doubts were long forgotten in the heat of the moment, and Lucas was the real-life version of her fairy tale Prince Charming once again.

Ten

In Love, Wisconsin

Sierra slid her long sarong off her legs and piled it onto the dock next to her. She sat down, and her left leg stretched across the width of the dock. She gracefully reached her toe out to touch the water. Kate, who was sitting right next to her, stretched her legs out as well and couldn't even reach the other side of the dock. Making a face, she pulled her legs up against her body and draped a towel across her knees. She leaned her head back against Alexis's lounge chair and let the sun warm her face.

"You look a little red." Kate cracked her eyes open—Sierra was leaning over her. Sierra pressed her thumb on Kate's shoulder and released it, testing for sunburn. "Yeah, you're red. Do you want me to grab the umbrella from my cabin?"

"I can get it," Kate offered. She'd been wearing SPF 30 every day since they'd arrived in Love, but still the sun had taken its toll on her bright white skin. "You're lucky you don't have to worry about sunburn, Sierra."

Sierra stood up, stretching her lean body. "Totally false," she said. "I get sunburned, but dark skin just doesn't show it as well. But I've been known to peel."

"Where is the umbrella?"

Sierra dipped her foot into the water, then said, "Um, I think it's in the living room, next to the futon." Kate set off up the hill, toward Sierra's family's cabin. When she returned a few minutes later, giant umbrella in hand, she was giggling.

"What's funny?" Sierra asked. Alexis peeked her eye open to look at Kate as well. She'd been napping most of the morning in her chair. She and Jake had been up until late the night before. In fact, Kate wasn't entirely sure Lex had ever made it to bed at all.

"I just fully walked in on your parents

making out," Kate said. She was still giggling, but was also mildly horrified.

"See what I've been living with all summer? At least they're getting along, but it's disgusting! They're all over each other all the time."

"Ew," Kate said, turning up her upper lip. She inserted the big sun umbrella into one of the holes on the dock and opened it, positioning it so she was shielded from the sun.

Alexis snorted, her eyes still closed. "Ew? You're not really one to talk, Kat."

"What?"

"You and Lucas were full-on making out in front of everyone a few nights ago at the blues fest. I thought you hated PDA."

"I do," Kate acknowledged. "I didn't realize he would want to spend the whole night making out. I figured the blues fest was a good chance for us to hang out and chill with everybody. Get to know each other, you know?"

"You know each other now," Alexis said, and chuckled. "Is he still the man of your dreams, Kitty Kat?"

"He's great."

Alexis perched herself up on her elbows,

lifting her sunglasses off her eyes to look at Kate seriously. There was a heavy pause before Sierra finally said, "Really?"

"Yeah." Kate looked at them suspiciously. "Why?"

Sierra dragged her toe through the water, avoiding Kate's gaze. Alexis blurted out, "Because he doesn't necessarily seem right for you, sweetie."

The pit that had been growing in Kate's stomach dropped like a bowling ball, dragging the remains of her insides along with it. She felt like she was going to puke. Her best friends, the people who knew her better than anyone else in the world, thought she was with the wrong guy. "Why?" she demanded.

"Kate," Sierra said soothingly, "don't take it the wrong way."

"Why can't you guys just be happy for me?" Kate said angrily. "He's totally sweet, and kissing him is the best feeling in the world. He makes me feel like a goddess, and he's excruciatingly hot. It's perfect, if you ask me." Alexis and Sierra both sat silently as Kate listed off Lucas's virtues. "And today I'm surprising him with a picnic out at the island, just the two of us."

Kate had spent all morning packing a picnic basket full of tasty treats, and as soon as Lucas came down to the dock, she was going to surprise him with a romantic outing. After their quasi-date at the blues fest a few nights before, the last few evenings had been spent around the bonfire with the whole resort crew. She and Lucas had snuck away a few times to make out, but they still hadn't really gotten any time to talk. He always found another way to spend their time together.

"So you really think he's going to give up waterskiing today to hang out with you on the island?" Alexis's doubtful tone frustrated Kate even further.

"Yeah," Kate retorted. "We talked about it last night. We agreed to spend the afternoon together." When she saw her friends watching her with true concern on their faces, she softened a little. She realized that if she could share her doubts with anyone, it was with Lex and Sierra. "The thing is, I feel like I hardly know him still. All we ever do is hook up."

"That's all Jake and I do," Alexis said, and beamed proudly. "But that's all I want to do. Have you guys noticed how *stupid*

Jake is? Geez. It's pretty much impossible to hold a full conversation with him."

Kate giggled. "Lex! That's terrible!"

"Seriously, though. He's not very bright."

"Okay, so that's what you're looking for this summer—but I want more than that."

"We know you do, Kat. That's why we're worried about what you're going to get with Lucas." Alexis perched her sunglasses up on her head, pushing her long bangs away from her face.

"All he ever does is water-ski," Sierra accurately pointed out. "He doesn't necessarily seem as interested in long afternoons talking and nights curled up together in a blanket under the stars as, say, *you* might be."

"I see where you're going with this, but you're wrong. Besides, after the blues fest we *did* sit in the boat curled up in a blanket under the stars. That counts!" Kate started to feel sort of desperate, realizing that she was trying to convince her best friends of her boyfriend's strong points—and she was having a hard time making her case. She had to admit that things weren't turning out exactly as she'd wanted them to.

Kate couldn't help but wonder if she'd

had impossibly high expectations about the summer she'd been waiting for all year. "I'm not ready to call it a lost cause," she finally said. "And I need you guys to stop questioning it, okay?"

Jake waited until Kate was comfortably situated in the back of the canoe with her picnic basket at her feet, then gave the canoe a push to guide it into the lake. "Have fun!" he called, and Kate could have sworn he was laughing as she clumsily dipped her paddle into the lake.

Kate looked at the empty seat in front of her, where Lucas should have been, and sighed. Less than an hour after her conversation on the dock with Alexis and Sierra, Kate had set off in search of Lucas. Despite the fact that at the bonfire the night before, they had discussed spending the afternoon together, Lucas had apparently decided to go waterskiing at a neighboring lake instead. She found him loading his gear into his family's car around lunchtime, which meant Kate's planning and packing had been all for nothing.

She acted as though she didn't care, and told Lucas to have a good time. He kissed her quickly as he hopped into the car. As soon as he pulled away, Kate decided to head out to the island for a picnic anyway, refusing to let a guy spoil her plans. It would be good for her to get some time to sit and think about things on her own, and she didn't want to spend the afternoon with her friends looking at her with I-told-you-so looks on their faces. Dipping her paddle into the water again, she felt the canoe tilt dangerously low to one side, and she cursed under her breath.

After spending this many years at a lakeside resort, Kate should have been far more adept at paddling a canoe by herself. But when she tipped the wooden paddle into the water, she realized that she'd always sat in the front of the canoe and let someone else steer. Adam had been that guy when they were kids, and Kate hadn't done a lot of canoeing since.

She dug her paddle through the calm lake water and attempted a C-stroke to steer the boat toward her favorite island. It was only a few hundred feet offshore, but it looked a million miles away as Kate struggled to turn her boat in the right direction while moving forward at the same time.

The canoe spun in several circles before

beginning to make progress away from shore and toward the island. Kate thrust her hand into the picnic basket at her feet and grabbed a handful of M&M's for sustenance. She needed the chocolate as fuel to make it the rest of the way to her destination. She was sufficiently embarrassed, as well, and was mildly relieved Lucas was out with the guys, since she knew she didn't look like the vixenlike water goddess she longed to be. She looked slightly more like a water bug, spiraling and spinning in frantic circles in the lake in her canoe.

After a few more large circles Kate finally straightened the boat out and paddled the rest of the way to the island with no further snafus. She was beaming with pride and self-confidence as she eased the front of the canoe up onto the little sandy shoreline and stepped out into the shallow water. After hauling her picnic basket up onshore, she grabbed the tip of the canoe and pulled the boat up onto dry land.

Not exactly the romantic picnic I had planned, she mused, pulling a woven blanket out of her basket. *Screw him*, she thought, suddenly angry at Lucas for dismissing their date and even angrier at herself for letting herself get so upset about it. She wasn't comfortable enough with Lucas yet to tell him how pissed she was, which frustrated her even further.

Kate shook the blanket and spread it on the ground under a tall pine tree. Needles had fallen off the tree and created a soft blanket on the ground. She lay down with the picnic basket at her side and closed her eyes, relaxing in the warm afternoon. She tucked her shirt into the underside of her bra, which allowed the warm breeze to float over her bare stomach.

"You look comfy."

Kate shot up, alarmed at the voice. She had been certain she was alone. There was no other boat onshore, and few people knew the island was a great place for a picnic. She had always believed this place was sort of her little secret. "You didn't look quite that relaxed in the canoe on your way over here."

"Adam," Kate groaned, yanking her shirt out of her bra and pulling it back down over her belly. She recognized the mocking, sarcastic voice even before he came into view from behind some bushes. "Just my luck."

"Hey, now." Adam looked hurt. "I'm just teasing."

Kate closed her eyes again and lay back on the blanket. "I know. It's been a crap day," she muttered. "I'm not really in the mood."

"There's always room for teasing, even in a bad day," Adam said, and grinned. "Right?"

"Your annoying comments? Not so appreciated today, okay?"

Adam sat, uninvited, and dipped his hand into Kate's picnic basket. He pulled out the loaf of bread she had packed, ripped a chunk off the end, and stuffed it into his mouth. "Mmm."

"You're a pig," Kate declared. "This . . ." She sat up and gestured toward her basket. "Not your picnic." She realized she was being especially abrasive, but after being ditched by one guy that day, she wasn't in the mood to deal with another. And a part of her still saw this as Lucas's picnic. Watching Adam eat it was making things worse.

"Come on, Kate." Adam looked at her seriously. "Don't take it out on me. I don't know what happened, but I seriously doubt it's my fault."

"Fine. Eat whatever you want. No one else is going to." Kate's mood was quickly souring. She had gotten up that morning planning to spend the afternoon alone with Lucas, and now she was stuck alone on an island with Adam. *Great*.

Adam munched on his bread. "Do you want to talk about it?" He asked so simply, so genuinely that she was tempted. It really seemed like he cared, but she knew he had an agenda. He was so bent on criticizing both her and Lucas, and she knew he was just fishing for something else to be rude about.

"Not really," she finally muttered. She knew Adam would be full of arrogant I-told-you-so's if she 'fessed up to what was going on.

"Okay." Adam started to stand up.

Without thinking, Kate grabbed his arm. "Stay," she insisted. She didn't know why she wanted him there, but she suddenly didn't want to be alone.

"I was just going to grab my banjo. It's in my kayak on the other side of the island." Adam smiled. "I thought you might like some music."

She nodded. When he returned a few minutes later, she had scooted over on the blanket to give him room. Though she was lying down with her eyes closed, she could feel him watching her. "What?" she demanded.

When he didn't respond, she cracked her eyes open and peeked at him. The look on his face was strange, an expression she hadn't ever seen on him. He was squinting in the filtered sunlight, but his eyes were firmly locked on her face. When he realized she was looking back at him, he blinked and coughed a little.

"Do you want some chocolate?" Kate offered, just to say something. Before he could reply, Kate blurted out, "Can I be honest about something?"

"In my experience you've been honest about everything," Adam said.

"That's just me."

"I know."

Kate relaxed into their easy banter. "I've never been good with the filter."

"Really?"

Kate sat up and narrowed her eyes playfully. "Are you being sarcastic with me?"

"Who, me? Sarcastic?" Adam grinned and pulled his knees up against his chest.

"I just don't like wasting time figuring out what people are really thinking. It seems to make more sense to just say what you have on your mind and move on." Kate picked at a piece of fuzz that was sticking out of the blanket beneath her leg. "If people are honest about what they're thinking and feeling and whatever, everyone knows where everyone stands. You avoid that whole level of confusion that's introduced into situations when people say things they don't really mean and then get upset when things don't work out the way they're supposed to."

Kate stopped rambling and pulled at the fuzz. It had pulled loose from the blanket and she twisted it around her finger like a tiny sleeping bag. Adam watched her fingers do their work and said, "So you're trying to tell me you're always honest and straightforward?"

"You don't think that's true?" Kate could sense Adam's disagreement in the tone he was using.

"No, I don't."

"Why's that?" Kate flicked the fuzz off her finger and watched it drift down to the ground and settle onto the pine needles.

"I don't think you're being totally honest when you're with Lucas."

"Whatever." Kate shook her head. Leave it to Adam to bring Lucas into this.

"I mean it, Kate. I was with you day and night all the way across the country, and I watched how you act around your friends and I've seen the real you."

"Oh, so you know me better than anyone, do you?" Kate rolled her eyes. Adam felt it was appropriate to analyze her now? As if.

"I just don't think you act like you when Lucas is around. You're sort of . . ." Adam paused for a second, apparently searching for the right word. "Blah."

"Blah? You're an asshole." He hadn't searched for the right word *quite* long enough.

"Not blah! Not blah," Adam said, and laughed. "That came out wrong. It's just that you don't seem like *you* when he's around. You're less feisty or something."

Kate sort of got what he was saying, and realized he wasn't trying to be entirely rude. So she decided to let it go. "Why do you dislike Lucas so much?" Kate asked this without really expecting an answer. But she couldn't stop herself from asking.

Adam paused, and his face turned toward hers in the pinkish afternoon light. For a moment he said nothing. When he did finally speak, his voice was quiet and deliberate, as though he'd taken the time to think it through for once. "Because he got the girl I'm falling in love with—and he's not treating her the way I would."

Kate's breath caught in her throat. She sat quietly, absorbing what he'd just told her. Adam must have taken her silence and stillness as the right sign, because he leaned toward her on the blanket and reached his hand out to touch her face. Just as his fingers brushed her jawline, Kate jumped up off the blanket and ran toward her canoe.

"Kate!" he called. "I'm sorry. I . . ."

Kate's legs were propelling her forward, even as her heart begged her to go back to him. *This is crazy*, she thought, and jumped into the canoe. She pushed her boat back from shore, and tears immediately sprung to her eyes. She could feel them rolling down her face the whole time she paddled back toward the resort.

As she approached shore, she could see Lucas standing at the end of the dock, ready to catch her canoe. Her emotions were already in a tailspin, and now she was spinning out of control . . . because half of her wanted to throw herself into Lucas's arms, but the other half wanted to paddle back to the island and find out what would have happened if she had stayed with Adam.

But now it was too late for that, and she couldn't stop the tears from falling.

Eleven

In Love, Wisconsin

For a few days after the island incident Kate mostly just holed away.

There was a permanent dent in their cabin's futon that resembled a less shapely version of her butt. She blew through three novels, and her sunburn had totally faded by the time she emerged from her hiding spot.

Of course, she hadn't been inside the *whole* time. She had spent plenty of time with Alexis and Sierra—who still had no idea what had gone down between her and Adam on the island—and every night at the group bonfire, Lucas was by her side. But ultimately Kate's main goal was to avoid Adam. She didn't have anything to say to him, and didn't know how to look at him after what had happened. More than anything, she couldn't explain her tears and had a hard time understanding why his eyes—the way they had locked on hers that day—were the first thing she saw when she closed her own.

The one time she had bumped into Adam around the resort, he had just acted like a slightly more distant version of himself. He didn't mention their day on the island, and it seemed like he was making a point of not coming to the bonfire in the evenings.

"Are you going to get your lazy butt off that futon and go outside today?" Gina asked, barreling into the cabin and fiddling with the tie on her halter top bikini. "Can you get this?" She nimbly sat down on the floor in front of the futon and thrust the ties of her swimsuit at Kate. "Hello?" She whipped her head around with an entitled look on her face, staring openmouthed at her sister. "What's wrong with you, anyway?"

"Nice, G," Kate said. "Your caring is so apparent." She tied her sister's bikini, then flopped back onto the futon.

Gina hopped up to sit next to her. "Seriously, Kate. You're a total bummer." She pouted dramatically. "Everything okay?"

"I'm fine," Kate said, convincing neither herself nor Gina.

"Is it Lucas?" Gina's eyes grew wide, preparing for the scandal.

"No."

Gina tilted her head, unconvinced. "It is."

"Seriously, Gina. It's not Lucas."

"Did you know Zack told Sasha he thinks I'm hot?" Gina giggled. "How cute would that be?"

"Lucas's brother?"

"Mm-hmm. We would be dating brothers!"

Kate scowled. "That's disgusting. Besides, G, all Zack does is water-ski all day. How does he have time for a girlfriend? Have you ever even spoken?"

"Oh, my God. Like you can talk! Lucas is, like, the leader of the ski crew. If it weren't for him, there's no way Zack would be out on the boat all day. Lucas is the one that's obsessed."

"And that's the problem," Kate muttered. Luckily, Gina was distracted by a bag of Doritos on the counter, and in her haste to open them and declare their deliciousness, she hadn't heard Kate's comment.

"The guys just got back from skiing," Gina announced, heading toward the door again. "Come down to the lake?"

"Fine." Kate shoved her book under the futon and changed into her suit. She grabbed a granola bar for the walk down the path, realizing she hadn't really eaten all day. *Nice*, she thought bitterly. *I'm totally losing it. What kind of idiot forgets to eat?*

Down at the dock she was relieved to see that Adam wasn't there. Kate's parents and their friends were loading into the pontoon boat for a cruise out on the lake. They went out most afternoons, spending the latter half of the day discussing thrilling research articles each had read, while drinking wine from a box. Kate waved at them, flashing a thumbs-up when her mom yelled out a reminder to put on sunscreen.

Kate hastily hid her granola bar in her towel after her mom turned to Gina with the comment that she shouldn't be snacking before eating lunch. (Gina had the whole family-size bag of Doritos on the beach with her.) Kate recognized that Gina's skating encouraged her to maintain a certain figure, but she felt angry realizing that her sister was going to have major food issues because of her mom's vigilant caloric observations. Luckily, Gina didn't seem bothered by their mom's nagging. She waved to acknowledge the comment but flashed her mom the middle finger from behind her bag of chips and then grabbed another handful.

At the boat dock Lucas and the ski crew were lounging around in the boat drinking sodas. A quick glance at the dock told Kate that neither Lex nor Sierra were around, so she sauntered over to the guys. Lucas came over to say hi, slipping his hand under her shirt to feel her exposed back. Kate shivered and backed away, embarrassed to have him touching her like that in front of everyone down at the lake.

"Hey," he said, pulling her close again. "Come here."

She gestured to the pontoon boat, which was still only a few hundred yards away, and said, "My parents . . ."

"Oh," he said, pulling back. "Right." He looked back at the other guys on the boat, and chuckled when one of them made a rude gesture in their direction. Abruptly Lucas turned to Kate again and said, "What are you doing tonight?"

"Um, nothing much."

"Let's go out, eh?"

Kate's face instantly broke into a huge smile. "Yeah, that'd be fun."

"We can grab some pizza in town."

"Sure." Greasy pizza at Romano's wasn't exactly the most romantic date ever, but it would be her and Lucas, alone . . . on a real date!

"We should be back in by about five. Wanna meet me by the barbecue pit around five thirty?"

"Yes," Kate said happily. This was major progress. Okay, so it shouldn't be such a major event having her boyfriend ask her out on a real date, but considering the circumstances . . . it was. Baby steps. And this was just what she needed to forget Adam and reconnect with the guy who really mattered.

Zack turned the key in the boat's ignition, gunning the motor to send up a roar of engine noise. It was Lucas's signal that the guys were all ready to go back out on the water, so Kate sent him on his way, planning their evening in her mind.

The lip gloss Alexis had forced on Kate was called Cherry Bliss, but Kate was anything but blissful. She was nervously licking her lips every ten seconds, and had licked off and reapplied the gloss so many times that she was starting to feel a little ill. Sierra and Alexis had helped Kate put together a perfect date uniform, complete with some sort of bronzing powder between her boobs that Alexis had dabbed on against Kate's will.

Kate was waiting on the steps of her cabin's small front porch, trying to look casual and demure. But instead she could feel the heat of the late afternoon sun baking into her skin and was paranoid the bronzing goop would be carried down her chest in a river of sweat. She pulled at her tight black tank top and tipped her face forward to blow into the dark cave of her shirt. Just as she was feeling cooler and more confident, she looked up and saw Adam standing a few feet away. She released the top of her shirt, embarrassed.

"Anything good in there?" he asked, nodding toward her chest.

She ignored his question and the amped-up fluttering of her heart in her chest. "I'm waiting for Lucas," she declared.

"Hot date?"

"Actually, yes."

"Nice." Adam nodded, then paused. "You look pretty."

"Adam . . . ," she warned. This wasn't the time to do this. "I can't . . ."

"Don't freak out," Adam said quietly. "I'm not trying to make you uncomfortable. You look beautiful, and I just thought you might like to know that."

"I don't," Kate said, tears welling up deep inside. They were too far from the surface to make an appearance, but she could feel them bubbling up. Any more comments like that and she'd be in trouble. Besides, the combination of dormant tears, Cherry Bliss, and nerves was making her insides queasy. "Please don't say things like that to me."

Adam looked at her seriously, then said, "Okay. I get it. Honesty only sometimes, right?"

At that moment Lucas came sauntering up. In his green polo, jeans, and sun-bleached hair, he looked like a male model. His hair was still wet from the lake, and she could see comb marks running through it. "Hey, bro," he said to Adam, glancing from Kate to Adam and back again. "What's going on?"

"I'm ready," Kate declared. "Let's go."

Lucas draped his arm around her. "See ya, Adam." He tugged at Kate's shoulder, steering her in the direction of the parking lot. They walked silently, and the gravel crunched beneath their feet as they trudged along. Kate was still trying to shake the feeling that had rocked her when Adam had appeared a few minutes ago. She was finding it more difficult than she would have hoped.

During the short drive into town Kate remained distracted, and she was much more nervous than she had thought she'd be. Lucas spent the whole drive telling her about that afternoon's wakeboarding showdown. "Zack and I totally creamed the other guys!" he declared proudly, thumping the steering wheel.

Kate tried hard to muster up the right level of enthusiasm. "Wow," she replied. "That's really exciting." He rubbed her knee absentmindedly. Kate hated the fact that it just felt sort of irritating.

When they got to the pizza place, Kate followed Lucas inside. She was still looking forward to their date, but was also starting to realize that maybe they would never have anything to talk about. At least he was making an effort. A date was a date, and it was exactly what she'd been craving. "Should we sit up here by the window?" she suggested.

"Nah," he said, shaking his head. "Not big enough."

She furrowed her eyebrows. "They're booths." The two booths in the front window could easily hold four people and several pizzas. How much was he planning to order?

"We need a table for eight," Lucas informed the waitress. Then he turned back to Kate. "The guys should be here in a few minutes. Turbo is slow getting ready. He's like a chick."

"Turbo? The guys?" Kate's face fell.

Lucas nodded, as though it was obvious. "Zack, Turbo, Johnson . . . the ski crew."

"Uh-huh." Kate could feel the frustration fermenting inside her, morphing into something horrible. *Chill,* she cautioned herself. *He never said it was a date. You just misinterpreted.*

She ordered a soda and waited patiently. Sarcasm dripped from her voice when she said, "I'm really looking forward to tonight."

Lucas put his hand over hers. "Me too." He didn't seem to get it.

When the guys got there, Kate felt even more like an afterthought—some sort of fifth wheel, unable and unwilling to discuss the merits of that afternoon's wakeboarding adventure.

She was a spectator on her own date.

When finally the last of the pizza had been consumed—capped off with a prize-winning burp, courtesy of Harris Johnson—everyone decided to head back to the resort for the bonfire. Kate hadn't weighed in on this decision, but she was pretty willing to do just about anything that would get her out of this one-on-seven date.

As an extra treat—something to make her date with Lucas even more memorable—they took Turbo and Nick in their car on the way back to the resort. Turbo spent the drive mooning people out of the backseat passenger window. *Nothing says romance like a fat, naked ass*, Kate mused.

Apparently Kate was living in a choose-your-own-adventure fairy tale, only someone else was making all the choices for her, throwing her into the parts of the story that should have been edited out. As Lucas pulled the car into the lot at the resort, Kate resolved that she would stop letting her heart be thrown around like this. Enough was enough, and Kate was tired of pretending this was paradise.

When they got out of the car, the bonfire was already in full swing. Sierra and Sasha were sitting on a log bench with Gina, roasting marshmallows for s'mores. Alexis and Jake were sitting with some of the kids who worked at the resort, singing along as Adam played his banjo.

It was the first night since their afternoon at the island that Adam had come to the bonfire. Kate suspected he had come out that night because he'd assumed she would be out on her date with Lucas.

Looking at him, strumming his banjo and cracking everyone up, Kate was struck with a sudden sense of longing. She longed to know what might have happened had she stayed that day on the island. And she longed for the "debates"—okay, arguments—they'd had on their road trip. More than anything, she missed their friendship.

He drove her crazy . . . in a good way, it seemed.

"Hey, Kat!" Alexis spotted Kate first, beckoning her toward her spot near the fire. "Back from your date already?" she asked, quietly enough so she wasn't screaming it out to everyone, but still loud enough for the people nearest them to hear. Adam was watching closely, so Kate squatted down right next to Alexis, out of his line of sight.

"Not a date, as it turns out," she whispered.

Alexis whipped around to face her completely and blurted out, "Shut up."

"I'm serious," Kate whispered again. "Pizza with the guys."

"Oh, Kat . . . Are you pissed?"

"Not thrilled," Kate admitted. "But I guess I'm not surprised."

Sierra sauntered over, a s'more in hand. "Dessert?"

Kate nodded happily, grabbing the gooey treat from her friend. The marshmallow stuck to Kate's lips. Kate leaned up against the log Alexis was sitting on and listened to Adam play for everyone. Sierra settled in next to her, resting her head on Kate's shoulder.

While Adam sang, Kate's mind wandered. But no matter how far it wandered, she kept coming back to one thing—the memory of Adam's face looking down at hers that day on the island. His voice floated over her now, singing Cat Stevens (or Yusuf Islam or whatever his name was), and when she glanced up, he was looking at her with the same expression again. But this time she didn't run. She looked back at him, watching the firelight cast shadows across his arms, making him look almost mystical in the smoke-filled sky.

Then the wind shifted, blowing a line of smoke straight at Adam, forcing him to break their gaze and sending him into a hacking coughing fit.

Kate averted her eyes, then felt a pair of arms wrap around her from behind. Lucas was lifting her off the ground, fixing Adam with the same look he had earlier that night, before they'd left for their "date." Lucas pulled her around to face him, and tipped her chin up toward him for a kiss.

It was the exact same marshmallow kiss they had shared at the end of last summer, but this time when Kate closed her eyes, all she could see was Adam's face looking back at her.

Kate pulled back and pushed her arms

against Lucas's chest to stop the kiss. When she turned, looking for Adam again, he was gone. Lucas was staring at her, clearly awaiting an explanation.

As Kate looked at him, then back at the spot where Adam had been sitting with his banjo just moments before, Kate wondered if it was too late to back up and get on a different path in her choose-your-own-adventure fairy tale. This one was all wrong.

Twelve

In Love, Wisconsin?

As often happened with true romantics, Kate's late-night confusion did not transform into daytime clarity.

She woke up superlate the next morning feeling absolutely awful. Her head ached, and her stomach felt ill. Whether it was from the mushrooms on the pizza or her emotional upheaval, she wasn't sure. But one thing was certain: She'd visualized her summer so clearly in her head, and nothing was going according to plan.

By afternoon she'd made herself insane thinking through her situation. It didn't help that it was a gloomy day and she was stuck inside. Of course, she'd heard the waterskiing boat motoring off early that morning. Only thunderstorms kept them off the lake, it seemed. Luckily, Gina had decided to join the guys in the boat that day, so she wasn't around to harass her sister.

The longer Kate sat staring at her open book, the more she realized she had completely lost perspective, and needed her friends to help sort things out. She threw her jeans on in place of her sweats, just in case, and rifled through the cupboards for a package of Oreos to bring along to Alexis's cabin.

Kate was fully aware that going to Alexis for romantic advice was about as reliable as picking the name of your future husband out of a hat—but at least Alexis was always honest, and introduced a little humor into situations. Sierra was as levelheaded and practical as anyone, so she'd surely have some solid suggestions.

Just as she was texting Sierra to ask that she meet up at Alexis's cabin, the door to Kate's cabin burst open and her two best friends came crashing in.

"Dish," Alexis declared bluntly, fixing Kate with a stern gaze.

Sierra threw a bag of Swedish Fish onto

the futon and settled in next to it. "*Why* is Little Miss Romantic glooming and dooming in her cabin all by herself?"

"Hi, guys," Kate laughed. "I was just coming to find you."

"I'm sure," Alexis responded sarcastically. "You've been holed up in this cabin all day. Annnnd, you were acting really weird last night at the bonfire."

Sierra nodded. "You took off without even saying good night. Not to mention the fact that the stars hadn't come out before you left. Our Kate never finishes her night before she can wish upon a star, right?"

"I'm not Pinocchio!"

"No, you're Snow White—waiting for your prince to come and sweep you away." Alexis snorted. "In the meantime, you're stuck with Grumpy and Dopey."

"As if that's going to happen," Kate muttered, grabbing an Oreo out of the bag. "You guys, I don't know what to do about Lucas."

"You mean, you don't know how to dump him?" Alexis grinned, bursting with pride.

"Hang on," Sierra cut in. "Which of us is Dopey? The other option is Grumpy?"

"They're the only two dwarves I can remember." Alexis shrugged.

Kate flopped back against the futon. "This is so not the point."

"You're right." Alexis settled into a cross-legged position on the floor and rested her chin in her hands. "We need to get back to the matter of you dumping your so-called prince."

Kate sighed dramatically. "Is that really what I'm supposed to do?" Hearing Alexis say it so certainly was depressing. Kate really did want to make things work with Lucas—she'd spent a whole year planning it out. "Why isn't it working?" she whined.

"He's kind of an ass," Sierra stated plainly. "To put it bluntly."

"You don't have anything to talk to him about," Alexis continued.

Sierra chimed in, "He brought friends on his date with you last night."

"And I saw Turbo's naked tushie," Kate said, and giggled. "Such a romantic way to end our date."

"You didn't tell us that!" Sierra covered her mouth with her hand. "Gross!"

"Listen, Kat," Alexis said, and fixed Kate with a firm gaze. "In all seriousness, if you're looking for romance and a Mr. Right that's going to treat you like Cinderella at the ball, you're looking down the wrong rabbit hole, so to speak."

"Enough with the Disney metaphors!" Kate cried out. "It's painful."

Alexis shrugged. "It's funny. But truly, Kat, I think we have a pretty good idea of what you're looking for, and you're just going to be disappointed if you keep trying to find it with Lucas. He just is not an even match for you. He treats you like you're fragile, a baby or something, when really you're the one who has to tiptoe softly around *him*. You can't be yourself with him."

Kate looked at her best friends. Sierra nodded. Alexis was right. Her analysis was spot-on, and she hadn't even made any sarcastic comments while delivering her message. "Unless"—Alexis's eyes gleamed—"you're just looking for a guy to hook up with, in which case Lucas is your perfect choice."

"No, Lex, that's you." Kate giggled, grabbed a couple of Swedish Fish, and then got serious again. "I need more than that. I want a future. I *do* want a prince."

"You're not animated, so a real prince is unlikely." Sierra grabbed an Oreo. "But you can find someone who wants a relationship, not just a set of lips."

"I need the emotional connection," Kate confessed. "I want a boyfriend who I also respect as a friend. One who is willing to give up waterskiing for, like, ten minutes to hang out doing something fun together." She looked down, studying a pinkish stain on the futon cover. It was shaped like a heart. Kate covered it with a Swedish Fish so she couldn't see it anymore. Adam's face suddenly flashed through her mind, and Kate was struck with the same sickly feeling she'd been suffering from all morning.

When Kate looked up again, she could tell that Alexis and Sierra had been watching her. "You'll find him," Sierra said quietly.

"I know," Kate agreed. Then she stopped. She wasn't ready to tell her friends what she was feeling about Adam, because she still didn't know what it all meant. And before she could think about a silly and unlikely crush on a guy she'd disliked for years, she had to deal with the relationship she was already in.

"So . . . what? No more hooking up?" Lucas looked at Kate blankly.

That night at the bonfire was the first

time Kate had seen Lucas all day. She had finally managed to pull him away from a burping contest with Turbo and Harris to talk to him about what she was feeling. Kate had carefully thought through the way she was going to word her breakup speech, but he'd cut her off right after she'd said, "I don't know if we're looking for the same thing with this relationship."

"Um." Kate was taken aback by Lucas's question. "Yeah, I guess no more hooking up."

"Too bad. You're still really hot." Lucas pushed Kate's hair behind her ear and looked at her with the same expression he had so many times before. For some reason the look had a lot less of an impact on her after those words.

Kate pushed his hand away from her head. She started to say something snippy, then realized that Lucas did have kind intentions. It was just that Kate had envisioned a very different summer romance than he had. That wasn't his fault. "It is too bad," she said finally. Then she leaned in and gave him one last hug. She breathed in the smell of sunscreen and lake water, letting the familiar scent take her back to that first kiss one last time.

As she stepped away, she noticed Adam near the bonfire with his banjo, but when he spotted Lucas and Kate together, he turned and walked back toward his cabin. Kate was relieved, since she didn't think she could handle anything more that day. Her emotions were in a rapid tailspin, and she had to get her head in order before she could let her heart lead her anywhere. And Adam seemed to have an ability to meddle with her emotions more than Kate was usually willing to allow.

Late that night, long after the last embers of the bonfire had died down and most people were in bed, Kate was startled awake. Gina was standing over her with her hands on her hips, her hair a tangled mess. "*Lucas* is at the window," she hissed.

"What?" Kate muttered groggily. "What window?"

"The window in *my* bedroom," Gina whispered. "He said he's looking for you."

Kate stumbled out of bed, quietly padding behind her sister toward the small second bedroom in their cabin. There was a tiny trail that ran behind their cabin, but no one ever used it. Frankly, it was sort of a creepy little path, and the fact that someone *had* used it made it even creepier. The lights were all off inside their cabin, so when Kate and Gina plodded into the bedroom, they could see Lucas illuminated outside by the silvery moonlight.

The window was open. Kate sat on the twin bed and said, "What do you want, Lucas?"

"Want to come out with me?" he said, with no further explanation.

"To do what?" she asked. Gina cleared her throat, suggesting that she knew full well what Lucas was looking for.

"I just thought maybe we could go down to the lake. . . . It's beautiful tonight." Kate wasn't stupid. She knew he just wanted to hook up. But it was sort of a romantic gesture—or would have been, if they'd still been together.

"Lucas, I can't," she whispered. "You need to go before you wake up my parents."

"Please?" he begged. The desperation in his voice made her feel sorry for him . . . and more confident about her decision that he definitely wasn't the right guy.

"It's just not going to happen," she said

bluntly. "I'm looking for a relationship, not a booty call."

Lucas shrugged, then turned to Gina, who was still lurking in the background, observing their conversation. "Do *you* want to come out and see the stars with me?" he offered hopefully.

"Ew!" Gina cried, covering her mouth as Kate slid the window closed and lowered the blinds.

The two sisters giggled hysterically on Gina's bed until their mom appeared in the doorway, demanding to know what they were doing up at that hour. Kate finally fell asleep in her sister's bed just before dawn, slipping into a dream where she was Cinderella at the ball. She woke up just as the glass slipper fell off her foot.

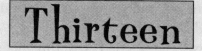

Thirteen

Love, Wisconsin

"Your parents are cute, Sierra." Kate squinted at the shoreline from her seat on the dock, watching Sierra's parents stroll along the beachfront holding hands. Sierra's mom ran playfully into the lake and splashed her husband with the cool water.

"I guess," Sierra said wistfully. "This is better than the fighting, right?"

"Of course it's better than the fighting. It seems like these few weeks at the lake have really helped them out."

"They've been going on so-called dates pretty much every night," Sierra said, rolling her eyes. "My dad keeps packing picnics to take on a hike, or taking my mom to the quarry to eat peanut butter sandwiches, or they go for milk shakes in town. It's like they're thirteen."

"I think it's great," Kate declared. "We can only hope we'll get that kind of romance with someone someday."

"Maybe *you* wish for that," Alexis said sourly. "I'd be horrified if someone tried to take me to the freaking quarry for peanut butter sandwiches. It'll take sushi in Tribeca—at a minimum—to win me over."

"Isn't it about the company?" Kate asked, leaning back in her beach chair. "Who cares where you are or what you're doing, as long as you're together?"

"Blah, blah, blah," Alexis said. "If it doesn't matter where you are or what you're doing, then why wasn't the waterskiing boat enough for you, dear Kat?"

"Come on, Lex." Kate smiled. "You know what I'm saying."

"I do, I do." Alexis lifted her sunglasses slightly so her eyes were peeking out from under the bottom of the lenses. "Speaking of waterskiing . . ."

Kate looked up. Lucas and Zack were ambling toward the boat dock, carrying their life jackets under their arms. It was already almost noon, so they were getting a late start. Lucas looked over at Kate and her friends but said nothing.

"What's that all about?" Alexis muttered.

"I hope he's a little embarrassed about last night," Kate said. She had told Alexis and Sierra about Lucas's attempted late-night booty call. "I feel bad about the breakup," she said, subtly watching Lucas load up the boat. "I really think I caught him off guard. I hope he's not too upset."

As soon as she'd said it, Kate wanted to reel her words back into her mouth and swallow them down again. Because Harris and Turbo had just walked onto the dock with a gorgeous brunette in a teal bikini— and Bikini Girl immediately wrapped her arms around Lucas's neck as though she'd been practicing for weeks.

"Didn't take him too long to move on, eh?" Alexis was clearly trying not to laugh.

"I guess not," Kate muttered. She was torn between wanting to laugh and wanting to cry. She'd spent so much energy over the past year planning out her romance with Lucas. She couldn't believe it could all shift, just like that. Of course, Kate had deliberately given up her spot inside those arms, but she hadn't thought Lucas would recover so quickly. He had moved on—without even a glance back.

The funny thing was, Kate felt completely disconnected from Lucas as well. It was clear, watching him with this gorgeous new girl, that she and Lucas were never meant to be together . . . not in the way she would have wanted them to be. Despite that realization, Kate still felt heartbroken somehow. Bizarrely, she was able to watch Lucas caress this girl's hair and nuzzle her cheek without even an ounce of jealousy. She just didn't care.

But Kate still felt hollow inside. There was something tossing around inside her stomach, and she couldn't make it stop.

"Kate, are you okay?" Sierra leaned over Kate, blocking the sun and getting right in her friend's face. "You're all white."

Kate nodded wordlessly.

"Do you want to go up to your cabin? Maybe we should get some lunch?" Sierra looked over at Alexis, the concern evident on her face. "Kate, seriously, you're freaking me out."

Alexis stood up, holding her towel out like a cape at her sides, blocking Kate's view of the boat dock. She was clearly trying to keep Lucas and his new girl out of Kate's line of sight. "I'm thirsty. . . . Let's go," she said, stretching her towel out farther.

"You don't have to block my view," Kate said quietly. "I don't care about Lucas and that girl."

"Why the hell are you acting like such a psycho, then?" Alexis whispered. "It's as though you just took a bite of the evil queen's poisonous apple and you're falling under her spell."

"No more Disney!" she cried, remembering her dream from the night before. "It's not Lucas," she repeated, watching carefully as Lucas got into the waterskiing boat and motored off with Bikini Girl and his ski crew.

Sierra and Alexis exchanged a look again. Sierra eventually said, "Do you feel like your romantic issues are still a little . . . unresolved?"

Kate blinked, caught off guard. "What do you mean?"

"Maybe it's time to figure out what's going on with Adam?" Sierra said this simply, without a hint of pressure.

"Adam?" Neither Alexis nor Sierra had

mentioned Adam in that way since they'd first arrived in Love. . . . Had she been that transparent?

"Girl, my cousin has been waiting for you to get rid of lame Lucas the whole time we've been at the lake," Alexis said, and ran her hand through her hair, twisting the bottom into a spiral. "You *have* noticed, right?"

Kate was suddenly covered in goose bumps, despite the heat of the sun beating down on her. "But the idea of me and Adam . . . It's nuts, isn't it?"

"It's perfect." Sierra smiled, nodding.

"You guys are hilarious together," Alexis seconded. "Not to mention the fact that he clearly worships the ground you walk on. Without being a total doormat."

"But he drives me crazy!" Kate declared. "And all we do is fight."

"It's romantic banter," Sierra said, and giggled. "You love it."

Kate flopped back onto her lounge chair. "But I've totally blown it with him!"

"I don't think so," Alexis disagreed.

"I have. . . . You guys, he told me he was interested in me, and I ran."

Sierra frowned. "You ran?"

"Literally ran," Kate said. "We were out

on the island, and he said he was falling in love with me, and I turned and ran like hell. I got out of there as fast as I could. It freaked me out, because I was pretty sure I was starting to feel something for him, too."

"Oh, Kate." Sierra sighed. Alexis was laughing, but covered her mouth as she always did when she laughed at inappropriate moments. "Have you said anything to him since?"

"Not really. He saw me before my pizza date with Lucas a few nights ago and told me I looked cute, but I told him not to say things like that to me."

"Oh, Kate." Sierra sighed again.

"Stop sighing!" Alexis demanded. "It's depressing. Kate, it's not a big deal. . . . If you and Adam had had a foundation built on politeness and appropriate responses, these little things would matter. But you've been completely honest with each other about everything, so it's not like he's expecting you to treat him like a porcelain doll emotionally."

"So what am I supposed to do?"

"Go get your guy!" Sierra declared. "Tell him you screwed up."

Alexis looked a little misty-eyed. "Do

you really think you might want to get with my cousin? There's something sort of sick and sweet about that, all at the same time."

"I don't know what's going to happen . . . but I know I need to talk to him to figure out if we're supposed to be together. When I see him, I'm pretty sure I'll just know."

"So stop sitting here and go find him," Alexis instructed. "You're a mess, and you're not going to feel any better until you get your issues with Adam sorted out."

"Do you want us to come?" Sierra offered.

"Would you?" Kate looked at both Sierra and Alexis, hopeful. It wasn't that she was afraid to talk to Adam on her own, but it was really awkward to have to go to his cabin, and potentially run into his parents, and then what if he had changed his mind and she had to walk back to her cabin all dejected and alone and . . . "Yes, please come with me. I need you."

"Well, let's go, then. We need to make this shit happen." Alexis snapped her towel at Kate and strode down the dock.

Kate jumped up and followed. She finally felt like she was back on the right path.

★

"Serious warning," Alexis said as they hiked up the rocky, slanted trail that led to Adam's cabin. "My aunt is chatty."

"Lex, I know your aunt," Kate responded. After all, they'd been coming to the lake with Adam and his family for years. She'd been around Adam's mom—Alexis's aunt— a million times at barbecues and down on the dock.

"You know my aunt publicly, where she understands the rules of social conversation." Alexis nodded. "On her own turf, she's something else."

When they got to Adam's cabin, Kate immediately understood what Alexis had been warning them about. Michelle, Adam's mom, welcomed the girls in with a wave of her arm and a mouth that was moving a mile a minute. She told them to "sit, sit, sit" at the table in their little kitchenette, and almost immediately had a cup of Kool-Aid poured for each of them.

Kate quickly surveyed the cabin, and surmised that neither Adam nor his brothers were there at the moment. It pained her to have to sit there and make idle chitchat with Adam's mom when all she wanted to do was find her guy and figure out where things stood, but she bit her lip and smiled while Michelle gave them her point of view on national politics. It was completely random, and Kate wanted to scream while sitting there patiently.

Eventually Alexis managed to squeeze a word in. "Aunt Michelle, you don't know where we can find Adam, do you?" Kate shot her a grateful look.

"Oh, of course you're looking for Adam, girls." She winked at Sierra. "But you knew he went home this morning, didn't you?"

Kate's stomach dropped straight down onto the ground beneath her feet. It felt like there was just a giant rotting hole where her insides used to be, and what was once her stomach was now just a pile on the floor of the cabin. "Home?" she squeaked out.

"Well, yes." Adam's mom nodded. "Adam's dad dropped him off at the bus station in town this morning. Apparently Adam got a text message from one of the other boys on the soccer team, and it sounded like they changed the practice schedule to start a bit early. Adam wanted to be prepared for the season, so he headed back to New Jersey."

"You sent him back alone? On the bus?"

Alexis asked angrily. Kate appreciated her friend's obvious frustration.

"He just decided to go last night—a spur of the moment sort of thing. You know Adam. . . . Boys will be boys. He caught a bus to Madison and will transfer to the express bus to New York later this afternoon. He's staying with the Blacks until we go home in a few weeks."

"What time did you drop him off at the bus station?" Kate whispered. Her voice sounded hollow, much like she felt. "Do you think he's still there?"

Michelle shook her head. "Well, no." She looked at the old classroom clock on the cabin wall, then down at her watch. "The bus left early this morning. He should be in Madison, if he isn't already on the bus to New York."

Kate stood up and thanked Michelle for the Kool-Aid. Sierra picked up their empty cups and set them in the sink.

Michelle followed them to the door, and called out after them, "Did you need to talk to Adam about something, girls?"

"Apparently not," Kate muttered. She looked through the trees and out to the lake. Kate could see her island poking out of the water, reminding her of the day when everything had changed. But Kate had blown it, and now she'd missed her chance to tell Adam that she was falling in love with him too. By the time they got back to New Jersey, too much time would have passed. "Let's get in the car," she said suddenly.

"The car?" Sierra queried.

"We're going on a road trip," Kate declared. "Let's finish this thing where it started. We're going to catch Adam on the road."

"That's my girl!" Alexis whooped. "But you know we'll have to drive faster than fifty-five if you want to catch his bus, right? Buses go slow, but not Kate-slow."

"If that's what it takes." Kate nodded, smiling. "True love takes sacrifice."

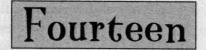

Fourteen

On the Road Again

"Dude, I've gotta pee." Alexis adjusted in her seat uncomfortably about an hour after they'd left Love. "It's serious."

"Lex!" Kate cried. "We don't have time to stop. We're already behind the bus by a few hours. We don't stand a chance of catching it anytime before Pennsylvania if we stop for a potty break."

"Okay, Mom." Kate saw Alexis smirk in the rearview mirror. "I'll just go in this OJ carton back here. If I miss at all, it's spraying in your direction."

Kate signaled to get off the interstate. "That's nasty, Lex."

Alexis shrugged. "I didn't get to go

before we hit the road. This was sort of a sudden trip."

"I'm being spontaneous. I'm not going to let Adam get away," Kate said, and pulled into the parking lot of a Perkins restaurant, just off the interstate. "I need to find him now—not when we get back to New Jersey in a few weeks. I need to know if we can be together, and I don't want to wait."

"How are you going to know?" Sierra asked, unfastening her seat belt to get out of the car.

Kate followed her friends into the restaurant. "A kiss will answer that. A kiss will tell me everything I need to know. I just hope he doesn't hate me for taking this long to figure everything out."

While Alexis and Sierra hit the bathroom, Kate bought a bag of muffins. She felt guilty for using a restaurant's bathroom without buying something, and figured it was the least she could do to thank her friends for coming with her on the road. On the way back to the car a few minutes later, Sierra dug into the bag and pulled out a lemon poppy seed muffin. Alexis requested a raspberry, and both were so engrossed in their snack that neither noticed the bus that was pulling into the parking lot as they were piling into their Ford.

But Kate did. Laughing, she said, "Look! It's the Q-tip tour!"

"What?" Alexis looked up from her muffin, muttering through a mouthful of crumbs. "What's a Q-tip tour?"

Kate put the keys into the ignition and backed out of their parking space. "The ladies from the bus trip. Remember, they were at the amusement park, and then we ran into them at our hotel outside Ann Arbor? Adam and I hung out with them playing cards?"

"That's so funny," Sierra assessed. "It's like they're stalking us."

The bus stopped, and the door opened. The three girls watched as some of the ladies climbed down the bus steps into the parking lot. Something kept Kate from driving away—perhaps it was the memory of her night with Adam, playing pinochle with Fern. Or maybe it was just that the bus tour reminded her of their road trip—when everything had seemed so much simpler, and her summer with Lucas was still just an imaginary and perfect scenario in her head.

They sat there so long, with Kate paralyzed and unable to move, that a car pulled up behind them and started honking.

Startled, Kate pushed her foot on the gas, then ground to a stop again when Sierra yelled, "Adam!"

"Adam is in that bus, Kate!" Alexis was waving her muffin in the air and had turned herself completely around in the backseat to look out the back window.

Kate looked in the rearview mirror. "He's with the Q-tip tour?" she wondered aloud. Sure enough, Adam was sitting in the back seat of the bus, staring absentmindedly out the window. His dark hair was immediately obvious, in stark contrast to the white heads bobbing around next to him. Kate threw the car into drive and whipped a U-turn, causing several cars turning into the parking lot to screech to a halt to keep from hitting them.

The sound of the squealing tires made Adam look their way, and he perked up in his seat when he saw Alexis's familiar little green Ford in the parking lot beside the bus. He stood up, and they could see him hustling down the aisle of the bus toward the front door.

Kate was out of the car in an instant. She met Adam as he descended the steps of the bus into the parking lot. Her heart was beating fast, telling her that her instincts had been right. She needed to be with Adam—she was sure of it. "Your hair is too dark for the Q-tip tour," she said, grinning when she saw him. "You're ruining the effect."

"I know." He chuckled. "Um, what are you doing here?"

"We're looking for you."

"Kate, listen," Adam said seriously, looking down to watch his own feet shuffling across the gravel in the parking lot. "I was on my way home . . ."

Kate nodded. "I know. Your mom told us. How did you end up here? Why are you on the Q-tip tour?" She was so confused, and mildly freaked out. This was surely some sort of sign, bumping into Adam in the parking lot of Perkins, back on the road.

"I got off the bus about an hour east of here and hung out for a few hours, waiting for a bus to take me back toward Love. I was chilling in a rest area, and out of nowhere, Fern comes up and taps me on the shoulder.

They were going my way and invited me to tag along, so I hopped onto the bus. I figured I could get a lift the rest of the way back from my dad or Alexis once I got a little closer to the resort—"

"But I thought you decided to go back to New Jersey for soccer practice. But now you're not—" Kate wasn't following. Adam was making no sense.

Adam cut her off to say, "There is no soccer practice. I just wanted to get out of Love. But I realized I'm not ready to give up yet."

"Give up?" Kate asked.

"I know you're with Lucas, but—"

"Not anymore," Kate said. She realized she should stop talking, since it seemed like Adam had something to say, and she was expertly ruining the moment.

Adam looked at her, hopeful, and started talking again. "I guess a part of me hopes that if I stick around long enough, maybe you'll realize that you're being a total idiot for not realizing that we need to be together."

"So why were you taking off on a bus back to Jersey, then?" Kate asked, grinning. She couldn't help but tease him, just a little bit.

Adam shrugged. "I don't know. I guess I just couldn't stand seeing you and Lucas together anymore. But it only took a few minutes on that bus before I knew I needed to come back and make a fight for it . . . for you." He paused. "Okay . . . in the interest of full disclosure, I have to admit that the bus was nasty. The dude sitting in the seat next to me was picking strings of something out of his teeth and sticking them to the bus window, like little stacks of hay or something. I didn't want to be there when they dried and started to fall off the window again." Kate laughed. "But that's not why I got off the bus. I wanted to come back for you. Kate, we have to try." He looked at her seriously, studying her face for a reaction, some sign that she agreed. "I know I drive you crazy. . . . I'll wait—the rest of the summer, next year—"

"Stop!" Kate said suddenly. "Enough. That's enough." Without another word Kate grabbed Adam's face and pulled him toward her. His eyes stayed fixed on hers as their lips connected, but then Kate closed her own, so she didn't know if he was still looking at her. She didn't think so. No one could kiss like that with his eyes open. She could tell that Adam was focused on their first kiss with every part of his body. It was electrifying, a kiss unlike anything Kate had ever felt before. The parking lot faded away, the loud roaring of the bus motor behind them became a low murmur in the background. All Kate noticed was Adam's body leaning into her, and the beating of her own heart.

She opened her eyes slowly as their lips pulled apart. His eyes were still closed. Kate smiled. "Yep," she said, still grinning. "That definitely feels right."

"Good," Adam said, smirking back at her. "I've been saving that one for you."

Kate rolled her eyes and jokingly said, "*How* is this going to work? We're crazy to think we can be together, aren't we?"

"I'm crazy about you," Adam said, pulling her into a hug. "And *you*—you are fascinated with my charm and subtle humor, correct?"

"Correct," Kate said, laughing.

Suddenly Kate became aware of their surroundings again. She waved to Fern, who was standing by the door of the bus. Then she pulled Adam into the backseat of Alexis's car. Sierra had already grabbed

Adam's bag from the back of the bus, and Alexis was in the driver's seat. They were ready to go.

As they merged onto the highway, headed back toward the resort, all Kate could think about was how romantic this scenario was. Kate and Adam's first hours together as a couple were on the road to Love. . . . She could think of no happier ending than that.

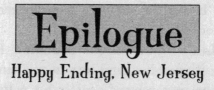

Epilogue

Happy Ending, New Jersey

"Hey, princess, what's going on?" Adam sauntered up and pinned Kate against the wall next to her locker, movie-star-style. It was the first day of senior year, and Kate was starting the year with a boyfriend. "Tell me I'm the guy of your dreams," he demanded in his mocking tone.

"I don't know about *that*," she joked, beaming at Adam. She laughed as he kissed her quickly. "Where's your locker?" she asked when he pulled away. "How far do I have to go to see my boyfriend between classes?"

"Right around the corner." Adam gestured toward the band hall. "In fact, if I remember correctly, it is in the very same bank of lockers you were in last year."

"Really?"

"Mm-hmm," Adam murmured, nuzzling her ear with his lips. They were still in that new-couple stage, and Kate loved it. "It's possible," Adam whispered into her ear. "It may be the very same locker, as a matter of fact."

Kate's heart started pounding harder as he slipped his hand into hers; a tiny slip of paper was pressed against his palm. She pulled their hands apart and twisted the piece of paper open. The words written on it were in her handwriting, and said: "hello, you, from kate."

"I found this in my locker," Adam said goofily, studying her face. "Look familiar?"

Kate smiled and held his hand tighter. "Yep," she confessed. "I left it there for you." Gazing up into Adam's smiling eyes, Kate knew for certain that she had finally found her prince.

About the Author

Erin Downing is a onetime book editor who now works at Nickelodeon. She spent a few months as a cookie inventor (but had to quit after she ate too many). Erin has lived in England, Sweden, and New York City and now resides in Minneapolis, Minnesota. She is the author of the Pulse Romantic Comedies *Dancing Queen* and *Prom Crashers*. Visit her at erindowning.com.

☆

Dear Coyote Courtship,
I've wanted to ask this girl to the Halloween dance all year, but I'm not sure if she even likes me. Should I talk to her friends before I ask her? Or should I just ask her?
    Sincerely,
    Confused Coyote

There were a million more Confused Coyotes.

Dear Coyote Courtship,
I really like this guy, but I'm afraid to ask him to the dance. I know he doesn't have a date yet, and he'd probably say yes, but I feel so intimidated. I am really shy. I'm afraid he'll get a date soon if I don't do something. Any suggestions on how to ask him as casually as possible?
    Yours truly,
    Chicken

And a lot of Chickens.

Hi, Coyote Courtship,
I really want to ask a friend to the dance,
but I'm afraid he might take it the wrong
way. How do I make it clear that I just
want to be friends?
    Thanks for the advice.
    Just Friends

Apparently several friendly coyotes hung
out on campus, because she read a few more
letters similar to Just Friends's.

The dilemmas were endless. Natalie Dean
never knew one dance could create such
anguish for so many people. She'd almost
rather take driver's ed again than read the pile
of letters from anonymous classmates that sat
in front of her in the campus newsroom. All
the letters were for the school newspaper's
column that she'd taken over when the for-
mer love columnist had quit.

The campus newsroom was empty. The
only sound was the hum of the computer
she was using and the occasional grunts and
shouts from the Coyote football practice
outside. Even though October was right
around the corner, it still felt like summer

in their suburban San Diego town, and the warm breezes wafting through the windows made Natalie want to take a nap.

She began typing.

The Coyote Chronicle
Coyote Courtship

It's the season of spooks, and we're all hoping to avoid messages from beyond the grave. With one of the biggest events on campus, Howl at the Moon, right around the corner, many of you are hoping to make this season full of fun rather than fright. I've received a lot of letters asking about how to hook the best date for the dance. *I'm dying to ask the one I've had a crush on all year, but I'm afraid. Should I take a friend? Is it okay to head to the dance with a group of friends? I want the one I've had my eye on all year to ask me; how do I get her attention?*

The fact of the matter is, I don't have a clue, and frankly I don't care because I wish I wasn't even going to this stupid dance, and anyone who has written in for advice should read their horoscope or contact Dr. Phil. My advice: Avoid love like the plague. Romance is confusing, and if you do think you ever happen to stumble upon true love, eventually you'll end up wondering if it's true or not.

Natalie giggled. She couldn't help it. It was hard to take the column seriously. When she'd first taken over the column, the idea of giving advice had seemed exciting. She'd never admit this, but it had kind of made her feel important and all knowing. At the time, her own love life had been going blissfully and she'd savored writing about romance. But lately the column had become a burden. Her relationship with her boyfriend was a source of anguish, and she was starting to feel as though she knew nothing about love when she was supposed to know everything about love. Worse, she'd even secretly been seeking love advice for her own love life via the Internet on a huge love advice website called Romeohelpme.com. Every time she sat down to work on the column, she felt like the biggest poseur.

She looked over her shoulder. School had been out for more than an hour and she'd been alone in the newsroom. However, paranoia always kicked in when she was screwing around, and she was private about her writing anyway. Her identity as the Coyote Courtship columnist was top secret. The only people on the entire newspaper staff who knew her identity were the newspaper advisor, Mr. Moore, and the editor in chief, Matt Logan. It was so on the down low she wasn't even supposed to work on the column at school, and she had to sign a contract with Mr. Moore promising that she wouldn't tell anyone except for her parents that she was the columnist behind Coyote Courtship. If she violated the agreement, it could result in her failure of the class. That's how seriously everyone took this column—everyone except for her.

The only reason Natalie was working in the newsroom today was because she'd been uploading too many songs on freebie websites and her computer at home had taken a hit from some kind of virus.

The first issue of the newspaper for the school year had hit stands a week earlier, which meant that new deadlines had been issued this week. A first draft of the column was due every Thursday after the previous paper hit stands. She'd sort of come to dread Thursdays for this reason. Love and romance were the most confusing topics on the planet for her right now. She'd rather solve equations than try to figure out dating and relationships, and she was supposed to be an expert!

She knew what all the fans of the column wanted to hear. She'd watched all the fairy-tale movies, and it wasn't like happy endings and blissful advice about romance were rocket science.

She glanced at the clock. She cracked her knuckles over the keyboard of her computer and chuckled. She was about to delete her fake column when the sound of skateboard wheels in the newsroom startled her. She swung around in her seat. Jeremy. Detention must be out. She wasn't sure what had surprised her more—the fact that he was a half hour early or the fact that he had skateboarded into the campus newsroom wearing a fireman's costume.

His dark hair peeked from beneath the edges of his hat; his deep-set eyes scanned the room. Jeremy wore his confidence well and he always seemed so secure in every new setting he entered. He was the only person she knew who had the courage to rip across campus in a Halloween costume as if he were in his backyard. Skateboarding on campus was so against the rules.

Jeremy's Ford Explorer was currently in the shop, and he was waiting for Natalie to give him a ride home from school.

"I've come to the rescue!" he announced as he glided over the floor, avoiding a stack of newspapers.

A million thoughts at once. What was he doing in the outfit? And he was early. She thought he had detention before the Halloween flea market. She was too worried he would catch a glimpse of her sarcastic column to find out. However, she couldn't help but notice how cute he looked. Really, he was drop-dead gorgeous in anything he wore, but the fireman costume really took his broad shoulders and deep, dark eyes to a new level. Even a cat would love to be rescued by him.

Her mind raced, and all she could think was to get her mouse to the close button or the minimize icon—whichever came faster. He was the last person she wanted to see her silly attempt to amuse herself. He had no idea that she felt so confused in their relationship, and this definitely wasn't the way she wanted him to find out. She hit minimize faster than her heart raced. The column disappeared.

"What's the matter with you?" he asked as he hopped off his new skateboard. He straightened out his fireman's hat.

"Nothing," she said a little too quickly.

He gave her a once-over. "You look startled and you're sweating."

"I am? I mean, hey, look at you!" She turned the focus on him. "Shouldn't I be asking what's up with you?" She put on an enthusiastic smile. "I know it's fire season in San Diego, but I didn't know you were signing on to help out."

He seemed excited by her interest. He tossed her a giant black-and-white ball of fur. "I just found these costumes at the Halloween flea market. Five bucks for both. I got the Dalmatian for you."

Natalie held up the giant costume and looked at a head-to-toe dog costume complete with a collar and tag that read BUSTER.

"Buster?" she mumbled. She didn't want to hurt his feelings, but this was hardly her vision for this year's Howl at the Moon.

The school held its annual Halloween flea market every year in the gym. It gave the students and staff a chance to recycle some old costumes. Natalie had skipped this year and sent Jeremy to see if he could find something cool for them, or just come up with ideas. She had no idea he would actually buy something without asking her first. He looked wonderful as a firefighter, but going as man's best friend was hardly what she'd had in mind for herself. Did he plan to lead her around on a leash? Not to mention it was eighty degrees outside and could hit the upper nineties on Halloween. This was San Diego. Visions of heat stroke danced through her mind.

"Try it on!" he urged.

"Uh. Well . . ." She searched for a reason to skip his suggestion.

"Bathroom's right next door," he reminded her.

"You want me to try it on right now? Um . . . it doesn't look like it will fit. It's a little large." For once her short frame seemed like a blessing. "Who sold you this?" she asked.

"Mrs. Green. She said it was her son's."

"Is her son Hurley from *Lost*?"

Jeremy laughed. "C'mon. Go try it on. It will look great."

"Let's just wait till we get home. I'll try it on at my house. There are better mirrors there."

"What's wrong with you? Don't be such a chicken. Go try it on."

Jeremy never understood embarrassment, and she doubted he'd experienced a self-conscious moment in his entire life. Always so confident, he felt comfortable in anything. He was daring and bold, and those were two of the qualities that had attracted her to him in the first place. Natalie had always felt safest tucked behind her computer working on a writing assignment. With Jeremy there was never a dull moment. He made everything seem so easy.

He grabbed her arm and yanked her from the seat.

"What if someone comes in," she said, "and I'm standing here in a dog costume?"

"School's been out for over an hour. Who do you think is going to see you? It will look great, anyway. Just go try it on. What are you waiting for?"

She stood there.

"Nat, no one is here. Just go." He whimpered like a dog. "Please."

She smiled. "All right. All right."

As she headed to the girls' bathroom, she reasoned that it was better to try it on now and let him see how ginormous it was going to be. Maybe he could even get his money back from Mrs. Green or try to sell it at the next Halloween flea market.

She went straight for the handicapped stall. She was afraid she'd get trapped in a regular-size stall. As she slid the outfit on over her clothes, she thought about the fact that people who worked at Disneyland got paid to wear outfits like this. She wouldn't take a king's ransom to wear this to Howl at the Moon. She was afraid to leave the stall and already felt her armpits growing damp. She almost tripped over the costume's legs as she maneuvered her way out of the stall. As predicted, she was swimming in the costume. She looked at herself in the mirror and didn't know whether to laugh or cry. She wanted to put her tail between her legs.

Mainly she was just worried someone was going to walk in and see her. The ears came down to her neck and she looked poufy. Her face looked like a tiny speck of land in the midst of a giant sea of black and white. For a moment she debated taking it off and explaining that it didn't fit. Leaving the bathroom and walking into daylight terrified her. She knew if she chickened out, Jeremy would never let her hear the end of it. Besides, he was her boyfriend and pretty much the only person she really needed to worry about looking cute for. He wanted her to wear it.

Natalie headed back to the newsroom. An ear flapped over her eye. As she pushed the ear away she heard laughter. Worse, her boyfriend wasn't alone. She faced her boyfriend and his best friend, Matt. Matt also happened to be the editor in chief of the *Coyote Chronicle*. She wanted to die. She sort of wished it had been anyone else.

"This is classic!" Jeremy shouted before succumbing to a no-breather.

Matt looked at her with a twist of sympathy and humor in his blue eyes.

Slowly she took a few steps forward. As she moved, she felt her tail take out a chair. She turned to her left to look at the chair, and when she moved, her tail knocked over something else. Judging from the shattering sound that followed, it was safe to say that whatever had fallen wasn't another chair. She was afraid to move and peeked over her shoulder. A pile of broken gray fragments lay beneath the tail.

"What was that?" She was afraid of the answer.

"Just Matt's ceramics project," Jeremy said in between peals of laughter.

"No. Are you serious?" She prayed Jeremy was kidding, but something told her he wasn't.

Matt tried to act like he didn't mind, but she sensed a shadow of disappointment in his eyes. He shrugged. "It's not a big deal. Just some dumb vase that probably would've broken when my mom put flowers in it anyway."

"It was a vase for your mom?" She felt horrible, and immediately crouched down and began picking up the pieces. "Maybe we can put it back together. I am so sorry. I feel terrible. I mean, was this something you worked on for a long time? This was special, wasn't it?"

Matt shook his head. "Nah, it was just some little school project."

"That he got an A on," Jeremy pointed out. "I don't think you're going to be able to glue two pieces of that back together." Jeremy's cell phone rang. Natalie was thankful for the interruption, and felt relieved when he turned away to answer it. He was only making her feel worse.

Matt crouched down next to her.

"Let me clean it up," he said. "Really, it's no big deal."

"Is there some way I can make this up to you?"

"It's okay, Buster." He smiled at her while on hands and knees.

She glanced down at the collar and tag around her neck and rolled her eyes. "Oh yeah." She felt self-conscious and awkward beneath his gaze.

Sweat trickled down her back as she collected pieces of the vase from the floor. Unfortunately, Jeremy was right. The vase looked like a pile of cookie crumbs.

"I should've never agreed to try on this stupid costume in the first place," she mumbled.

"You look hot," Matt said. She paused to glance at him. "I mean, not that kind of hot." He quickly corrected himself. "The hot where you sweat and you want to cool down. Not that you aren't hot or anything . . . I mean, just never mind. You know what I mean."

Interesting that he was the one stumbling

over his words when she felt like the fool. Not only was she crawling around in a dog costume that was ten sizes too big, but she didn't normally hang out in the newsroom to begin with. He was probably dying to know what she was doing here.

They threw handfuls of clay fragments in the trash, and Natalie felt horrible with every toss.

She never worked in the newsroom.

"I was working on the column," she blurted out. "I didn't have a chance to tell you and Mr. Moore that my computer at home is broken, but I have a deadline on Thursday." She tried to sound nonchalant. "My brother's fixing my computer tonight. So I won't be in here anymore after that. I mean, I'll be in here for newspaper stuff . . . just not to write." She was babbling now, and she prayed he didn't ask to have a sneak peek at the column.

"Okay." He ran his fingers through his curly hair. "If your computer breaks down again, you can always borrow mine. I don't care if you come to my house. It's better than someone finding out who you are."

"Thanks. I would've borrowed Jo's but she has a paper due."

"How's the column going?" he asked.

"Don't worry. I'll have something in time for the Halloween issue of the paper."

Matt shrugged. "I wasn't worried. With you, Nat, I know I never have to worry."

If he only knew how ironic that sounded to her. She'd much rather be writing about the lack of vegetarian choices on the cafeteria menu, or even writing the cafeteria menu, for that matter. Or other things she felt passionate about, like, what was the whole point of algebra? Someone had yet to explain this to her. Really, what was the point? And why did she have to understand the meaning of the little letter x?

Matt put his hand on her shoulder. "Thanks for taking this on, Nat. You're doing an awesome job, and I really couldn't picture anyone but you doing this."

She forced a smile. If he only knew the truth.

Want to hear what the Romantic Comedies authors are doing when they are not writing books?

Check out **PulseRoCom.com** to see the authors blogging together, plus get sneak peeks of upcoming titles!